JUNIOR LIFEGUARDS

Oscar Season

JUNIOR LIFEGUARDS

BOOK
TWO

Oscar Season

by

ELIZABETH DOYLE CAREY

DUNEMERE
Books

NEW YORK • SAN FRANCISCO

PUBLISHED BY DUNEMERE BOOKS

ISBN: 978-0-9984997-1-0

JUNIOR
LIFEGUARDS

Oscar Season

Wake up!

"**S**elena! Time to wake up, *mi amor!*"

My mother waltzed into my room, snapped up the shades and flicked on the overhead light. Despite the contrast between her morning-person energy and my night-owl sleepiness, the day started out friendly enough, even though I'd stayed up way too late watching movies on TV while texting my bfs.

"Mami, it's vacation, remember? I get to sleep late today!" I grumbled. Then I rolled over and tugged the covers over everything but my ear, because I was hoping to hear profuse apologies and the sound of the shades rolling back down.

But who was I kidding? Apologies and rolled-down shades might have come from someone else's mom, but not mine. (Note to self: buy one of those eye-masks like the old time movie stars wore.)

My mother moved around my room, efficiently snapping shut the tubes of beauty products on my dresser, rattling the hangers as she re-hung clothes in my closet, dropping my pens into my pen cup with a sharp *tap, tap, tap!* It was a symphony of "Wake up!" noises with a melody of "You're messy!" floating on top like an accusation.

"Selena, come! There's no time for late sleeping today. We have only a little while this morning to get organized before I have to work. Get up, get up! And *ay,* this room! It's a pigsty! It's hurting my eyes!"

I like things a little messy because it makes my room feel cozy and lived in, while my parents' room is so clean, I bet you could perform surgery in there and not need to sterilize it first.

"Mami, leave it! You don't have to clean all the time. You're not at work yet!"

Uh-oh. Did I just say that out loud? I pulled the pillow over my ear at last, knowing what was coming next.

"Selena Diaz! How can you be so spoiled? I wish I didn't have to clean all the time, especially at home. But do you think you would remember that when you're throwing your things everywhere? No!" And on and on she went.

Whenever my family fights, we fight in English. My mom and dad are all Spanishy when they're happy—all their endearments and praise filter through the sweet and gentle words of my early childhood in El Salvador. *Amor. Tesoro. Milagro. Corazon.*

But when they're mad, they're American.

I lifted the pillow off my ear so I could gauge where she was in her rant.

". . . and find you a job!"

"A job!" That wasn't part of the usual rant! I ditched my covers and sat upright in my bed. "What do you mean? I already have the Junior Lifeguards thing in the afternoons that Papi's making me do, plus the extra swim class they say I have to take, and I'm getting tutored for math, which I'm dreading. Now I need to get a job, too?" One day out of school and this was already the worst summer of my life. And we were in Cape Cod—summer vacation paradise! Ha!

"Yes. Of course," she persisted. "Now that you are thirteen you can earn a little of your pocket money, no? I got your working papers already from the school, so let's look at the classified ads, because you can't just sit around during your free time this summer like last year. You know, when I was your age . . ."

"Ack!" That was all it took. Every time she launched into how hard it was for her growing up in El Salvador, and how easy we American kids had it, I had to escape. I jumped out of bed without even checking my new phone (a reconditioned iPhone I got for my birthday a few weeks ago), and ran into the bathroom to take my shower. Even with the door closed and the water running I could *still* hear her ranting on, all in English, about how spoiled American kids are, with our Instagram and lattes and the Mashpee Commons mall.

In the hot shower, I rested my head against the tile and took a deep breath. It's not like we asked to move to America.

I still remember when I was really little, back in El Salvador. I'd loved it. We'd lived on a big ranch with all my cousins and aunts and my *abuela* and *abuelo*; all the dads were already in the U.S., making money. It was so peaceful and fun; there had always been someone around to braid my hair or slip me sweets or watch the elaborate plays and performances that we'd put on all the time. No one pressured us: there hadn't been all this talk of grades and careers. Everyone had looked like me, and my mom had been softer, more relaxed, more patient. But here . . . well. It's all about success and goals. Every night when I go to kiss my mom good-night, she is either studying for her accounting exam, ironing a mountain of laundry with starch (some ours and some from the big house), or reading a self-improvement book (thinking of more ways to torture me, I'm sure).

I missed the old days. I struck a tragic pose in the shower, like Katherine Langford in that *Thirteen Reasons Why* show that my parents won't let me watch, and I tried to really pay attention to my posture and how my body felt in that moment of grief. I made sure I'd be able to call on it for some future performance onstage. Then I rinsed out my conditioner and turned off the water.

Dwelling on the past wasn't going to get me anywhere; we weren't going back to El Salvador, at least for the foreseeable future. Anyway, I wasn't even sure I wanted to.

So for now, I had to get into character. Acting was what I loved and what I used to tackle life's dramas: in tough moments, I'd create a role in my mind and play it out.

Who knows? Maybe someday my acting skills would win me an Oscar and I could go back and buy my *own* ranch in El Salvador!

Costuming is very important in acting. Today I had decided to play the role of "responsible American teenage job-seeker" to calm my mother down a little. I slid into my seat at the breakfast table wearing a nice pair of long, plaid Bermuda shorts and a cute pink polo shirt with scalloped sleeves. I am pretty short, but well-proportioned, so I am choosy about what I wear and how well it fits me; my mom does a lot of alterations for me by hand.

My father was running out to a job site so he planted a kiss on my head and grabbed a cup of espresso my mother had brewed for him. "You look so *bonita, mi amor*," he said proudly. "Ready for summer."

"Thanks, Papi," I smiled.

My skin is kind of always tan and I love makeup and potions, but today I went bare-faced and wholesome (which my parents prefer). I have long dark hair that is thick and gets kind of reddish in the sun. I usually put it in rollers and make it huge and wavy, but today I was wearing it very flat and conservative, with a little barrette at the side. My mother looked at me approvingly as she set down my mug of *horchata* (a kind of Salvadoran Ovaltine she orders online) and handed me the *Cape Cod Times* and a highlighter.

"Selena, what time does Junior Lifeguards start? What do you need for the course? Where do you meet?" She peppered me with questions as she moved around the kitchen; she seemed to be assembling dinner ingredients.

I glanced at the newspaper but my fingers itched to pull out my phone so I could check in on all my feeds and see what my celebs and friends were up to, and let my public know what I was up to, even if it was not much.

Instead, I remained focused and in character.

"I don't know yet," I said. And then, "Oh, Mami! Are you making *pupusas* for us tonight for a treat?"

"No, *mi amor*. These are for the girls."

Of course. Anything for "the girls." I poured

myself some cereal and began eating it grimly while half-studying the help wanted ads.

"The girls" are the Frankel sisters, Alessandra and Samantha, ages eleven and thirteen, who live in the mansion on the dunes, a few hundred yards from here. Their parents employ my mom and dad, as cook/head housekeeper and landscaper/ property manager. The house we live in is the Frankels', too: it's the estate's caretaker's cottage. The Frankels live in London (Mr. Frankel is a rich Israeli business mogul and Mrs. Frankel is a glamorous African news reporter), so when they are not here on the Cape, which is usually fifty weeks of the year, we have the property all to ourselves: the beach access, the pool, the trampoline, the vegetable and flower gardens are all ours. It's amazing! I like to pretend I'm a movie star and lie on a float in their pool with a cold lemonade.

But this year, the Frankel girls came with their boy nanny Nigel for the whole summer, and everything is different. I'm losing my free run of the property. I won't be able to have my friends over because who wants to just sit in my tiny bedroom or on our little scrap of yard? And what if we run into Samantha while my friends are here, and she tries to boss me around? It gives me shivers just to think of it.

"And Selena, speaking of the girls, you must be kind to Samantha at your lifeguards training today. She won't know anyone so you include her, ok?"

"Ha!" I nearly choked on my cereal. *Kind to Samantha? Me?* "Mami, trust me. She doesn't want to be seen with me, the hired help." It was my mother's brilliant idea for Samantha Frankel to do Junior Lifeguards this summer. I was furious when I found out.

"Selena, for shame saying such things. Think of Eleanor Roosevelt!" scolded my mother. She likes to quote the former first lady, who supposedly said "No one can make you feel inferior without your consent." I only half-understand what that means or even how it applies to me. And why should I have to be nice to the Frankels who have everything?

Here's the deal, the Frankel sisters, Samantha

and her younger sister, Alessandra, say hi if we run into each other on the property when we're home, like when I dress up to help my mom serve at their parents' parties or when I'm bringing starched laundry up on hangers on the golf cart in the morning or whatever. They always remember my name (or someone reminds them of it before they get here). It's just that we all know it's like they are the masters and I am their servant and I only live here through the good graces of their parents and the hard work of mine. But we do not hang out or pal around off the property. Like, in summers past, if we were to see each other in town or at the movies, we would just look away. It's easier. We all understand the rules. I don't want them messing with my life and they don't need me in theirs.

That's why Samantha didn't acknowledge me at the Junior Lifeguards try-outs last week. To be honest, I didn't acknowledge her either. I'm sure she thinks I'm beneath her so she doesn't want to be seen speaking to me, and that works for me. I don't need any social overlap with Samantha Frankel. Only my best friends know my living situation and I'd rather keep it that way. I like it that people assume I live on Brookfield Lane because I'm rich. When I post pictures of myself floating in the Frankels' pool on a raft, I caption them *#summer* and *#capecod*, not *#employerspool* or *#maidsdaughter*. It's doesn't hurt anyone to let them think it is my house. And if people don't think I'm rich, well, at least I don't want them to think I'm someone's maid. The bottom line is this: the less my path crosses with Samantha Frankel's, the better.

"Now, *mi amor*, tell me what you see in the paper for jobs," said my mom, deftly patting down and flattening the pupusas without even having to look at them.

I sighed and took another bite of my cereal. Skimming the columns, I tried to see if there was anything that looked promising. "Driver needed, driver, delivery truck driver, bartender, road crew, hotel chambermaid . . ."

"No!" said my mom definitively. "No cleaning."

"That's most of what's available for kids my

age, Mami," I said. "Especially without a driver's license."

My mother tossed her bobbed hair. "We didn't move to America for you to be a maid! What else?"

I rolled my eyes. I wanted to say, *"But you're a maid,"* but my mom would have bitten my head off. My parents' jobs are a means to an end, but their ambitions for me and my brother Hugo are massive, like, the American dream.

My dream is to be a major movie star, like Reese Witherspoon or Indigo Darling, and I work hard to build my brand by maintaining my social media accounts, blog and website, as well as keeping up my talents and my looks as much as possible. Junior Lifeguards wasn't something I wanted to do this summer, but since my parents are making me do it, I am looking on the bright side. It will get me in better shape and sharpen my swimming skills, which will just make me more employable in Hollywood later (I'm thinking roles in lifeguard movies, shipwreck movies, anything set on a beach . . .).

I skimmed the paper again. Plumber's Assistant, Dental Hygienist, IT Systems Manager, Chambermaid at Motel, Chambermaid at Hotel, Maid, Maid, Maid . . .

Briskly, I folded the paper and pushed it away from me.

"Anything?" asked my mom hopefully.

"I'll find something," I said grimly. "Don't worry."

After I helped my mom fold the clean sheets and towels for the big house, I updated my Facebook, Instagram, Twitter and Snap, and then rode my bike to the library. The morning was sunny but still chilly; typical June-in-Cape Cod weather and a preview of the beautiful days to come.

My bike tires were covered in sand after a few blocks, and it sprayed up on my legs as I rode, sticking to my ankles, but I didn't mind; it made me feel summery. Early dew-spangled roses climbed fences and trellises outside the neat little houses in town, and though I wanted to snap off one big bloom to put behind my ear, it didn't fit with my costuming choices for the day.

I parked my bike in the rack on the grass outside the library, and checked my phone one more time. There was a text in my group chat, BESTIES, which comprised me and my friends Jenna Bowers, Piper Janssens, and Ziggy Bloom.

"RISE AND SHINE! Ready to rock it today, girls? #brave #strong #wewillsaveyou." It was from Jenna, who basically made the rest of us try out for Junior Lifeguards.

I smiled. Even though I was nervous about the lifeguarding program, I was psyched to hang with my friends on the beach all summer. It was better than what my father had originally wanted, which was full-time summer school.

"CAN'T WAIT!" I lied. Then I silenced my phone and went inside.

The main room of the library was buzzing with activity this morning as usual; there was a line for check-outs already and adults on every computer in the lobby area. I was ten minutes early for my tutor orientation meeting, so I put my stuff down in a corner and went to the children's room to see if the library cat was around.

I would love to have my own cat like my friend Jenna does. I would have a fluffy golden one and I would name it Oscar (like the Academy Award) and it would sleep on my bed and wear a thin leather collar with a little bell on it. But my parents won't let me have one because our house is not really our house and they don't want some cat roaming the property and bothering the Frankels when they're here. We have lots of little restrictions like that, which are imposed only by my parents and not by the Frankels, but that doesn't make it any easier.

"Hello there!" the librarian greeted me. It was unusually quiet in the children's room today. The puzzles and toys were stowed neatly in their bins, the computers sat unused, and the only noises were the tick of the clock and the soothing burble of the huge fish tank.

"Hi," I smiled but I felt a little shy since I was the only one in there.

"I'd love to help you find anything you need," said the librarian, smiling warmly at me.

"Is the cat here?" I asked quietly.

She laughed. "That's an easy one! He's right here in his bed next to my desk." She waved me over to peek.

The library cat is orange-and-white striped, skinny and small, and super-mellow. He was curled into a ball with his chin on his paws, fast asleep in his little round bed.

"Cute!" I said softly. "Can I take his picture?" I asked, whipping out my phone. This would be a great meme—an "I hate Mondays" picture of a cat asleep.

"Sure!" said the librarian.

I snapped the shot, quickly posted it, and put away my phone. "Can I pet him? What's his name again?"

She smiled. "Harry Potter, of course!"

"Oh, that's right!" I laughed. I bent down

and smoothed his head with my fingers. His eye-lids fluttered but he stayed asleep. "Hi, Harry," I whispered.

"He loves kids," said the librarian.

"I guess he'd have to if he lives here. And books, too."

She smiled. "We just had a big group in for the early story hour and he was the star of the show, so now he's all tuckered out."

"Do they chase him around?" I giggled, picturing it.

She nodded. "It's kind of chaos. The idea is that parents or caregivers can drop the kids with me for an hour or two while they browse in the library or even run an errand or go to the gym or something, and then they come back and pick them up. Harry and I get a little overwhelmed some days, depending on who shows up."

"I think little kids are hilarious. How many come?"

"Hmmm, today there were five but I've had as many as ten. You never know, because it's just drop-in."

"Oh my gosh. Ten kids!"

She grimaced. "Rainy days in August are the craziest."

We both laughed at that. Cape Cod is summer vacation paradise, so when the weather is bad the visitors are desperate. Our town is crazy crowded on rainy days because all the people who would normally be at the beach descend on the two main streets, looking for things to do. Parking is nuts and the lines at the nearby movie theater and the deli and even the checkout counter at the library are insane.

Harry stretched and yawned and opened his eyes to look at me. Then he rested his paw on my hand and went right back to sleep. The librarian laughed again.

"Look at him! He likes you! What's your name?"

"Selena Diaz," I said.

"I'm Janet Hayden. It's nice to meet you, Selena. So are you looking for a book?"

I shook my head. "No, I'm just here to do an

orientation with my tutor. I *am* looking for a job though. Isn't there a bulletin board here, for jobs and stuff?" I stood and looked around the room.

"Yes, the job board's right over there by the door. I also keep a babysitter list here at the desk, if you'd like to be on it."

"Sure, thanks!" I gave her my contact info, peeked at the job board and found nothing except a landscaping job.

"Selena?" Janet called across the room to me. "I was just thinking . . . Might you like to work in the children's room in the mornings with me? I have a little fund for 'special projects' that I can use at my discretion so I could pay you. It's not much money, but it's something. And you'd certainly pick up some babysitting jobs from it."

"Really? Are you serious? I'd love it!" I said, incredulous. "That would be so great. Thank you! I do have my tutor on Tuesdays and Thursdays from ten to twelve, though."

Janet smiled. "That's okay. So what if we say Monday, Wednesday, and Friday mornings from nine to noon? I could pay you . . . ten dollars an hour? Is that fair?"

"That would be amazing. I would love it! Thank you so much!"

Janet put out her hand to shake. "We've got a deal, then. I'll see you Wednesday!"

"See you then! And thanks! I'm looking forward to it," I grinned and gave Harry one last tickle and trudged out to look for this tutor dude.

What had started out as the worst day ever was starting to turn for the better. I couldn't wait to post about it on Instagram. Maybe a meme of the sun coming out from behind the clouds . . .

Action!

I stood at the front desk, notebook and erasable pen in hand, waiting for my new tutor, Martin, to appear. The earlier rush had cleared and there were only a few people ambling through the main room, and one young guy with blue hair who was reading a beat-up old paperback in one of the wing chairs, a backpack at his Converse-clad feet.

Sighing, I glanced at my watch. I was still a minute early, but now that I was here, I just wanted to get it over with. I knew the tutor would be a total geezer and nerd so all I could hope was that our sessions would help get my parents off my back and maybe make me a little bit better at algebra.

I craned my head to look out the window and see if anyone might be coming up the path. My dad had found this Martin person through his friend who is an assistant principal on the Outer Cape so I was looking for a professorial type or an old guy. My father had also found him some other job to make it worth his while to come up here to tutor me. I think the Martin guy had even given my father a break on his usual rate because of the other job my dad got him.

Suddenly, the guy in the blue hair lifted his head as if waking from a dream. He looked around the room, zeroed in on me and said, "Selena?"

My jaw actually dropped and he smiled and began to gather his things.

"Martin?" I said incredulously.

This guy was way younger and way cooler looking than anything I had imagined. He walked over, smiling broadly, and put his hand out to shake.

I forced the shock off my face and dialed up

a megawatt movie star smile to hide my initial surprise.

"Nice to meet you," I said.

Martin was laughing. "I know, I don't look like a math tutor, right? I'm actually a computer geek, a coder, whatever you want to call it. I'm getting my PhD in computer science at UMass."

I had to laugh too. "Yes, you are definitely *not* what I was picturing."

"I booked us a tutoring room on Level Two, so let's head there and we'll do our orientation and then make our summer plan. We'll going to have fun and you are going to get great at math. Don't worry!" He waggled a finger at me.

I never thought there'd be a way to make math fun, but Martin was great. It turns out he's really into theater and acts at a community playhouse in Wellfleet. He's also been down to New York to see lots of shows on Broadway because his friend is a stagehand there, so we bonded about theater for our first ten minutes. He promised to bring me some scripts he's collected and said that as a reward for my hard work, we can sit outside and read a scene from a show at the end of our sessions on Thursdays.

"Okay, for today, I just want you to plow through these worksheets so I can get a sense of where you are and what your gaps and weaknesses are. Then I can design a custom curriculum around that to start with tomorrow."

I sighed heavily. "Now for the boring part. Nothing personal."

"With all due respect, Miss Diaz, I think you will find that once you have the proper tools, math is anything but boring!" Martin smiled and did jazz hands at me.

"We'll just have to see about that," I joked.

Our hour together flew and before I knew it, it was time to go.

We exchanged contact info and I entered Martin into my phone.

"Are you on Snap?" I asked as I typed. I'm

always collecting followers and trying to build my brand.

Martin laughed and shook his head. "Nah, I can't stand that social media stuff. I'm kind of funny that way. That's why I prefer theater to movies. It's about the authentic experience." He tucked his phone into his pocket and hefted his backpack onto his shoulder.

I was confused. I looked at him sideways as we left the room. "But I thought you were a computer guy?"

He shrugged. "Even though I love computers and games, it's more about the storytelling for me."

"Social media is kind of storytelling," I offered, strolling slowly down the stairs.

"I guess. It just seems like self-promotion to me most of the time. And a lot of work to keep up with. No offense," he said with a genuine smile. He held the door for me as I exited the stairwell.

"I don't mind. I couldn't live without it. It's how my friends and I all communicate and how I keep up with the world." I wanted to add, *"And how I let the world keep up with me,"* but I suddenly felt embarrassed.

"As long as people keep it in perspective, it doesn't bother me. I just can't imagine what world those Kardashians live in."

We both laughed. We'd reached the lobby.

"I'm parked out back. Do you need a ride anywhere?" he offered kindly.

"Nope, I've got my bike out front, but thank you. And thanks so much for today. It was more fun than I expected," I said.

"Thanks. We will have a good time and I promise you will improve at math. I'll see you tomorrow with your customized curriculum, for our first official session."

I dropped my bike at our back door and raced inside.

"Mami! Mami! Are you here?" I called.

I looked around the first floor. The washing machines and dryers were humming along but she wasn't home; she must've been up at the big house. She never minds me going up there to find her, but with the Frankel girls here now, there was no way I'd go up there.

Back in the kitchen, I spied a note from my mom on the counter.

"Back at 1:30. Lunch in fridge. Good luck, mi amor! Besos! *Mami."*

I opened the refrigerator. Inside was a small platter of pupusas, covered in Saran Wrap. A sticky note on top said *Selena*.

This day was getting better by the minute! A job, a math tutor with blue hair and a taste for drama, and now a delicious homemade lunch?! I felt like Anne Hathaway in *The Intern*—a modern woman successfully juggling her happy full life.

My phone vibrated and I pulled it out to see who it was and a picture of Jenna was smiling up at me.

"Hey, Jen," I said, shutting the fridge with my hip and carrying the platter to the counter.

"What's up, sister?" said Jenna. "Psyched for lifeguarding?"

I sighed as I preheated the frying pan and added a little butter. "I guess."

"It's going to be great. I think we should all try to get there early, just to get the lay of the land, you know."

I glanced at the clock. Thirty-five minutes. "I'll try. I just got home and I still need to eat and change. Guess what? I got a job at the library!"

"*Whaaaat?* Paid?" said Jenna, incredulous.

"Uh-huh," I bragged.

"Awesome, girl! Good for you!"

"Thanks." I gave the frying pan a shake to distribute the butter, then I dropped three pupusas in the pan, where they sizzled and crackled and began to release their delicious cheesy aroma. "Let me eat now, okay? I've still got to run and change and get my stuff. I'll try to be early."

"Okay. I'm calling the others, too. See you there."

"*Ciao!*"

Before I ate the pupusas, I snapped a pic and posted it with the hashtag *#gourmetlunch* and three smiley faces. Then I wolfed down the food, scrawled a thank you note to my mom and cleaned up. I gathered all of the things I needed for my new role as Beach Lifeguard (trainee): my pretty beach towel printed with big flowers, some fancy tinted sunscreen, a pink hairbrush, hair elastics in a rainbow of colors, cool sunglasses I got with my saved birthday money, fun little flip flops from Target, all to tuck into a pretty beach tote of my mom's. I snapped a pic of all my supplies, posting it as *Junior Lifeguard props.*

I had my required red one-piece on under my beach dress. Bud Slater, the strict program director of Junior Lifeguards, had made it very clear the other day that bikinis were a major no-no for lifeguarding (Samantha Frankel had shown up for her try-out in a white one! I was embarrassed for both of us but so glad it wasn't me—not that my parents would let me wear a bikini yet anyway), and red was the only suit color allowed. I'd have to wear this hideous sporty suit every day for the rest of summer. No one in Hollywood would be caught dead wearing something like this. I checked myself out in the mirror again and sighed again, then I took a selfie and posted it with the tags *#juniorlifeguards #brave #strong #wewillsaveyou*. Branding finished, I put everything in my tote and hopped on my bike. Ten minutes until the starting time; I'd be early as Jenna had requested.

I pedaled down the groomed gravel driveway and took a right out onto Brookfield Lane. As I drew near the corner I avoided looking at the final house on my right. It's a big mansion, white with black shutters and incredible gardens surrounding it. I'd recently learned that it belonged to my good friend Ziggy's grandparents, only . . . Ziggy doesn't even know she has grandparents, let alone that they're apparently zillionaires living in our very own town. I'm certainly not going to be the one to tell her but I had to tell Piper and Jenna the other day. It just felt like the plot of a movie come to life, like *The Princess Diaries* or something.

I took a right onto Ocean Avenue and pedaled toward the bike rack at the crest of the dune. There were lots of bikes already jammed in there, which made sense. It was the first official day of summer vacation and probably every kid in town was there to soak up the sun and celebrate their freedom, whereas I felt like I was now going to my jail sentencing!

I parked my bike and locked it and headed to the office at the big wooden beach pavilion to see where the Junior Lifeguards were meeting. My palms were sweating; I tried to calm myself by getting into my "California lifeguard" role.

"Hey kid!"

I looked over. It was my brother Hugo cleaning up tables post lunch rush. He works at the Clam Pot, which is the snack bar and beach shop on the pavilion here at Lookout Beach.

As I watched, he found a beach toy that a family had just left behind. He chased down the departing mother, who took it gratefully from him. Then he returned to what he was doing just as I reached his table to say hi.

"Hey," I said. "I got a job!" Hugo has never had any problem getting or keeping jobs. He works all year round, even during school, and he volunteers at the church and the food pantry. My friends and I call him Saint Hugo.

He reached up his plastic-gloved hand to high five me. "Awesome! Doing what?"

I winced as I high-fived his sticky hand then I filled him in on everything.

"Cool. Mami will be happy. We'll celebrate tonight when I get home from the movies." Hugo's night job is as a ticket-taker at the theater.

"Lifeguards now?" he asked.

I nodded and glanced around. "Yes, but I'm not sure where . . ."

"Down there," he pointed to a big group of kids standing by the lifeguard stand. "You'd better hustle. They've been there a while."

"Oh no! Bye!" I hopped off the pavilion and scrambled across the sand to join the group, glancing at my watch. It was only twelve fifty-seven; I still wasn't late. How come everyone was already there?

I reached the group in time to hug my friends hello (I'm a big hugger), and I spied Samantha Frankel out of the corner of my eye but pretended I hadn't. From what I could see, she looked amazing in her new red bathing suit. Her long, thin legs were endless, unlike my stumpy ones, and the red suit really popped against her dark skin.

I scanned the group to see which boys were there and my eye fell on Hayden Jones, tall, broad-shouldered, and tan-skinned like me. He was standing off to the side a little, but I caught his eye and smiled at him and he smiled back.

And then it was starting. Bud Slater clapped his hands and called, "Alright everyone, time to begin the first day of the rest of your lives."

Bud was in his fifties, ropy-muscled and of medium height, with short-cropped, bristly grey hair, steely blue eyes, a deep tan, and a permanent slash of zinc oxide on his lower lip. He always wore a collared shirt and a pair of red lifeguard board shorts, as well as a silvery whistle on a lanyard around his neck. My drama teacher at school would have been thrilled with Bud's ability to project his voice. It could reach any corner of the beach, any time, in any way he wanted: scolding, angry, cautionary, warm. I had never realized before I met him that a strong voice was such an important life-guarding tool.

Bud enjoyed being the center of attention and seemed to like giving mini-lectures whenever he could. Like, right now.

"Today we will begin to make you into guards. Every day, we will break into groups for our warm up and training, then you will be assigned to different town beaches for the second half of the afternoon to apprentice under the senior guards. If you don't have a bike, we can get you where you need to go and back here again after the five o'clock closing. Groups will change weekly, so do not worry if you are not with your friends. It may be intentional." He smiled wickedly.

Please let me be with at least one friend, I hoped silently. I could only get through this if I was with my squad.

Bud continued. "Training is not meant to be easy. In fact, it will be hard. You will be expected to dig deep and try your best. Lives are on the line every day at the beach and lifeguards must be in peak condition to handle all of the possible challenges, both mental and physical. If you are not yet strong, we will make you strong."

Dios mio. I am not yet strong, but I wasn't so sure I wanted to be made strong.

I glanced uneasily at Piper. She felt my glance and looked back at me, grimacing. Piper is strong and physically able—she works on her family's horse farm pitching hay and handling the huge horses—but she is a landlubber like me. I felt like I was in the wrong place and my urge to flee was huge; it was like I was at a casting call for a part that was all wrong for me. I dreaded the humiliation of trying. Oh, why had I let Jenna and my parents talk me into this?! My palms felt cool and tingly and my stomach clenched.

Bud continued on, introducing the senior guards who would be helping with training today,

and outlining our regimen, which involved cal-
isthenics and interval training, group trust work,
equipment training, skills, and a brief lecture on a
lifesaving technique or protocol. Can something be
difficult *and* boring?

Before I knew what was happening, Bud started
carving the crowd into groups. Quickly I posi-
tioned myself right next to my besties and found
to my relief that he lumped us all together. Maybe
this wouldn't be so bad after all, I thought. If I was
with my friends, I could probably handle anything.
And please, just no Samantha Frankel.

But at the last second, Bud said, "And one
more!" and shooed Samantha over to join us.

I pretended I didn't notice. I didn't want to be
her lifeline *or* her servant, and I could easily see
either happening. To avoid having to interact with
Samantha, I pulled my phone out of my tote bag
and called, "Okay, girls! Team photo! Everyone
get in!"

"Hey!" Bud's voice cut sharply across the
beach. "No phones. Ever!"

My face burned as I tucked the phone back into my bag.

"I was going to say something," whispered Phoebe. "I knew he wouldn't like that."

"*Awk*-ward!" singsonged Ziggy quietly.

Jenna just gave me a dark look, as if she was annoyed I'd cast a shadow on our group right out of the gate.

"Sorry," I said, my face flaming. I set my bag aside on the sand and avoided looking at Samantha. Now I felt like *I* was the interloper and I was extra-humiliated that she had witnessed that. I'm sure she was thinking, *Leave it to the maid's kid to get it all wrong.* Of course, she said nothing, just looked away.

Bud came around and handed out a sheet of exercises to the kids who would be team heads; naturally Jenna was ours since she is a swim team star and Team Captain of our Junior Lifeguard class. I braced myself for more scolding, but instead Bud said calmly, "Emergencies are called into central dispatch by walkie talkie. Any other

kind of phone on the beach is a distraction for lifeguards and if I see them in a guard's hand anywhere on the beach, it's grounds for dismissal.
That goes for trainees as well. Not your fault just
now, but now you know."

I gulped and nodded and all of my friends
looked elsewhere to graciously avoid staring at my
reaction. I wondered if Samantha was looking at
me, though, and the thought of her doing so made
me just want to curl up and hide.

When Bud walked away, I exhaled.

Jenna scanned the sheet and then said, "Okay,
listen up, people!"

Piper and I shared an amused glance; Jenna was
born for this. She loves being in charge and she's
super-competitive and sporty.

"We're going to start with some sprints to warm
up. Then we'll move onto bear crawls, burpees,
push-ups, sit ups, and lunges. Then some more
sprints. It's called interval training and it's great
for calorie burning but also for cardio training. Alright?" Jenna dragged her heel across the uneven

sand, creating a starting line. Then she walked about a hundred yards away and did the same to create a finish line. She returned to us and laid down her sheet with a rock on it to hold it in place.

"We're going to run as fast as possible to that far line then back to here. When I say go, go. *Go!*" she yelled. It caught me by surprise and I was slow taking off.

Jenna and Piper bolted ahead and Samantha was right behind them. Ziggy trotted along at a speed that could only be called "half-effort," but I went for it. My legs are not long like the other girls', but I when I put my mind to it, I can move. I pumped my arms and ran as fast and hard as I could. I just didn't want to come in last.

After a few of those, in which Jenna and Samantha appeared to be racing each other, Jenna checked the sheet again.

"Now. Let's do the bear crawls," said Jenna.

Piper groaned. "Can't you let us skip those?" she whispered, looking over her shoulder for Bud.

"No. They're good for you," said Jenna firmly.

Bud had picked the right person to lead our team. I never would have made my friends do all this.

"Um, what's a bear crawl anyway?" I asked.

Jenna dropped on her hands on the sand, then, with her butt popped up in the air, she staggered along the beach alternating walking with her hands and feet.

I had to laugh. "Ha ha, Jen. Seriously."

Jenna stood and briskly wiped the sand from her hands. "Seriously, what? That's a bear crawl."

"But your *behind* is in the air!" I whispered. Everyone giggled. I glanced at Samantha's face to see if she thought it was funny but she was looking away, maybe checking out the boys across the beach.

Jenna gave me a stern look. "It's excellent conditioning. We have to do it. No one's looking at my butt."

I giggled. "Well, no one may be looking at your butt, but I hope people are looking at mine!" I gave a little wiggle, and all the other girls laughed again, except Samantha.

"Right, then. I'll start," said Samantha, not even cracking a smile at my joke. She dropped to the sand and began shimmying along the beach, butt in the air.

O-kaaaay. The rest of us looked at each other and my face burned at being so totally ignored. Then Piper shrugged apologetically at me and dropped, and so did the others. I was still standing there, paralyzed.

"Everything okay over there in Jenna's group?" came Bud's piercing voice.

"Here goes nothing," I whispered aloud, then I dropped, praying that none of the boys were looking.

Bear crawls are hard. Bear crawls on sand are ridiculously hard. By the time I reached the turn and was heading back, everyone but Ziggy was standing there, finished, panting. Awkwardly I scrabbled back toward them, standing up early and lumbering over the finish line on foot at the end. Jenna raised her eyebrows at me but I chose to ignore her look of reprimand, and dusted my hands off as my lungs heaved and my muscles burned. I was sure Samantha was thinking, *Gosh, the maid's kid is so out of shape.*

"Now sprints again!" trilled Jenna. "Got to get that heart rate back up!" she added.

"Good," agreed Samantha, as she took her place on the starting line again.

Jenna smiled at her and Samantha smiled back.

Ugh, all I need is for those two to become friends! Talk about awkward. Jenna coming over and passing me in the yard at my house as she heads up to the Frankels'? Jenna sleeping up there at the big house and my mom cooking them breakfast? Yuck. And what if Jenna told her that we always jump on her trampoline and swim in her pool, and that I sometimes post pictures of us there on Instagram that imply it's my own house?

Annoyed, I flung myself between them for the next sprint, daring Samantha to acknowledge me. When Jenna called, "Go!" I put my head down and ran with all of my might.

Still, though, I was three strides behind them

as we came into the final stretch after the turn. I did beat Piper, though, but I nearly threw up in the process. This time it was me with my hands on my knees, gasping for air afterward.

"Okay, burpees!" called Jenna.

"Ooh, good one!" said Samantha, clapping. "Lets *do* this!" she cheered. She and Jenna high-fived. I dry-heaved, thinking now how *pupusas* were a terrible thing to eat before training.

"Can't we take a little break?" I begged.

Jenna's face clouded. "We just started, Leens."

"I know, but . . ." I looked around at Ziggy and Piper for support, but they, too, looked at me blankly. "Okay," I said, humbled.

It went on like this for half an hour: with me getting weaker and more frustrated by the minute, and Jenna and Samantha getting happier and closer by the minute. They looked like stupid cheerleading partners. And still, Samantha hadn't even looked at me.

I was about ready to break down when Bud finally waved us all over. "Okay, kids," he bellowed.

"Thank God," I muttered. "Finally!"

We gathered around him and once everyone was there he cried, "Now for a jog!" He spun around and bounded down to the water's edge and began jogging along on the firm sand.

"Seriously?" I wailed.

There were some other groans like mine, but shockingly, most of the kids fell into line right behind him. My feet were planted firmly in the cool sand as I stood there wishing I was in a movie right now—it would have this whole training session as a quick montage of scenes: me struggling, me almost quitting, me learning to overcome, me getting strong and triumphing! And it would only take about one minute of screen time.

Oh, why can't life be more like the movies?

"Come on, Selena," whispered Piper. She grabbed my hand and pulled me with her. "Jenna's being a pill and the Samantha thing is super-weird, but if you keep up it won't be so bad, okay?" She gave my hand a squeeze and ran on.

Jogging along the wet sand, dodging the small

rocks and jingle shells that studded the water's edge, I did the only thing I could think of to make myself feel better. I began to sing out loud.

3

First Encounters

"We are the lifeguards, the mighty mighty lifeguards, and everywhere we go-o, people want to know-o . . ." I sang quietly at first., but it inspired and distracted me and the rhythm helped me keep pace. As we ran, I worked my way through a few verses of the song. Jenna kept turning her head around to shoot me dirty looks, but I pretended not to see her. I didn't care. I had to do something to make myself feel better.

I don't want to brag but I have a good voice.

The one time I really feel totally relaxed and confident is when I'm singing. It's like the whole world just melts away and I only feel the warmth of the song in my chest cavity, spreading through my shoulders and stomach and lifting me up like a hot air balloon. Sometimes at home, I set up my phone and record myself singing a song; then if it's good, I'll put it on my YouTube channel. I get likes from strangers and that's how I know I don't stink. One of my dreams is to record a song and post it and get thousands of likes.

After the third verse, a few of the kids ahead of me, like Hayden Jones and a girl called Summer from my history class, began to join in on the chorus. Then a few more kids joined in. By the fifth time through, Jenna popped out of the line and jogged back to me.

"Stop, Selena!" she huffed.

"Why?" I asked. I knew I was being a little feisty but I didn't care. Bud had put me in my place with the phone thing. Then I'd done all his awful exercises and suffered through like ten wedgies in the process, and now it was my turn to have a little fun. It wasn't like I was disobeying him.

"It's disrespectful!" said Jenna.

"Since when are you Bud's little minion?" I huffed, glaring at her. I hate it when Jenna gets super-bossy like this. It often happens when we stay up late at a sleepover and she wants to go to sleep while the rest of us are still having fun and making noise.

She glared at me. "I just think you're looking for trouble," she said coldly, and she left the line to jog back to her place.

"Whatever," I said. And I started up again. "We are the lifeguards, the mighty mighty lifeguards . . ."

We jogged along the water's edge for a bit. The wet sand was cold and squishy and hard to run on. Occasionally I'd fail to spot a rock and I'd land on it awkwardly, my heel adjusting for it at the last second so as not to drive my whole weight onto it and hobble myself. The sky was blue with a few streaky clouds on the horizon, and the beach was empty once we moved past the lifeguarded area, which was designated by a roped swimming area and two flags placed equidistant from the lifeguard stand in either direction.

When we reached the jetty, Bud stopped, which surprised me.

"Guards," he began (he wasn't even winded, *btw*). "A lot of what you will do on the beach this summer is about rituals and systems. Put good rituals and systems in place, and they make your job easier and help everyone stay safe. One ritual I always do is a survey run before a shift. I like to jog in both directions along the beach, survey the crowd, look for trouble-makers—like teenagers playing chicken, or adults who are drinking alcohol. I look for any beach issues, like the remains of a bonfire that might not have been put out, or dead fish washed up or signs of red jelly fish. I like to get a sense of what the water's doing, and the wind. And most of all, I like people to see me. I'm in my red shorts, I am a guard, I am claiming my beach. That's how I see it. All of my senior guards do this before a shift. It warms you up, it puts you in touch with your environment and your customers, and it focuses your senses. Got it?"

We all nodded.

"Questions?"

No one said anything.

"About the singing . . ." he began.

Everyone's head whipped to look at me. I could feel my face flushing a little, but I tried to hold Bud's gaze. I briefly flicked my eyes at Jenna and she was shaking her head at me slightly so I looked away, back at Bud.

"Yes?" I said quietly.

"I like it!" said Bud, pointing at me. "Keep it up!" And he turned and began his jog back to the other end of the beach. Kids looked at me, some in admiration even, as they jogged past me. Jenna narrowed her eyes and looked away, and of course, Samantha didn't even glance at me.

"Good job, Leeny," said Ziggy, patting me as she jogged past.

As the end of the line assembled, I fell into place

at the back, and began my song again. "We are the lifeguards, the mighty mighty lifeguards . . . !"

Well, at least I can put my own spin on things here, I thought. *I might not have strength or endurance, but I do have talent!*

With our warm-ups done, Bud doled out the beach assignments for the day. He paired me with Piper and sent us just up the road to Crescent Beach with a senior guard. Jenna and Ziggy he kept with him. I wasn't bummed to get a break from Jenna and I was hugely relieved that I wasn't stuck with Samantha. I shuddered to imagine spending an afternoon with her at the beach, with her ignoring me, or worse, me trying making small talk ("So do you prefer your whites bleached or just spot-treated with OxiClean?").

"Yay!" said Piper, coming to join me.

I linked my arm through hers and squeezed. I was so happy to be partners. Piper was tall, tan and strong, with her long hair in a thick braid. In her red suit, she already looked like a guard. I was proud to be seen with her.

"Let's go get our stuff and ride over," I said.

Walking up to grab our bags, Piper said under her breath, "How's it going with the princess?"

Piper's such a sweetie. She's super sensitive so she always notices how people are feeling and she hates to see people upset.

I rolled my eyes. "I think we've each decided to pretend the other doesn't exist."

Piper widened her eyes at me. "What? That's weird. Do you think you can keep that up all summer?"

I shrugged, acting like I didn't care either way, but I'd had the same thought. "I don't know but what's the alternative? She becomes friends with all of us and we hang out at her house while my mom vacuums around us? Or we become enemies and she makes her mom fire my mom and then I'm homeless?"

Piper looked pained. "Hmm. I guess I can see what you mean."

"The less contact, the better," I said, setting my mouth in a grim line. But I, too, had my doubts about how we could sustain the silent treatment in such close quarters.

Crescent is a shallow beach, mostly for little kids—especially on weekdays—so Piper and I had a pretty quiet afternoon, thank goodness. The most action we saw was when a toddler ripped off her diaper and squatted to poop in the sand. It was so disgusting but also kind of hilarious. Piper and I were shrieking and laughing and the mom was just standing there looking helpless because, well, it was just too late to do anything but let the kid finish.

Our senior guard, Jessie, sent us to get a shovel and a plastic bag from the supply shed, and then we trotted over to the mom who was apologizing like crazy and also kind of laughing. She had to chase the kid to deal with the cleanup, so Piper and I opened the garbage bag and debated who was going to do the scooping. We got laughing so hysterically that by the time we regained our composure, the mom was back and dealt with it all, even putting away the shovel and throwing away the mess.

When we got back to the stand, Jessie was laughing, too.

"That doesn't happen every day!" she cried. "I promise!"

"Yeah, right," said Piper. "Add that to our job description: pooper scooper!"

"It's worse if you guard at a pool. There are lots more 'situations,' if you know what I mean!" said Jessie.

"Ugh. Then it's ocean all the way, for me," I said.

Jessie spent the next couple of hours telling us lots of funny (and sometimes gross) lifeguarding stories and she also gave us a bunch of advice that sounded great but was hard to remember. Then, suddenly, it was closing time. Jessie showed us how to take down the flags and where to stow them in the shed, and how to rope off the lifeguard stand so no one climbs up it at night (even though that's *all* anyone does at the beach after hours).

We hopped on our bikes and pedaled back to Lookout Beach for closing time. All of the Junior Lifeguards were back, comparing notes on how their shifts went. I was just so grateful that I hadn't needed to dive in and save anyone today that I stayed silent. I felt like such an imposter with my weak physical skills and could only pray that I am not physically tested in this program anytime soon. Today's training session had highlighted how much work I need to do.

Bud gathered us together and gave a little speech.

"Great first day, kids. I like the enthusiasm and the energy. Keep up the good work. It might not be a bad idea to keep a journal or a list of things you learn—just write it down when you get home at night and it will help you remember. Back here tomorrow, same time and place. Thanks for coming!"

Everyone began to drift away. Jenna was being standoffish with me and I saw her look for Samantha, but Samantha had already bolted for home, using the dune path that led to the beachside entrance to her house. (I would definitely not be using that entrance this summer, even though I usually did in the off-season.) I intentionally turned away from Jenna. She'd been so self-righteous today and full of herself. I hate it when she's like that. I wondered if she planned on making Samantha her NBF. *Good luck,* I thought.

Up ahead was Hayden Jones. He looked so fine in his red board shorts and a worn-in, slightly clingy white tee shirt with some school name on it. He was already tan and his hair was getting lighter by the day. I jogged to catch up to him, ready for a break from the group dynamics of the day.

"Hey, did you like the first day?" I asked.

Hayden smiled. "Not too bad, I thought. You?"

I shrugged. "It's not really my skill set. I mean, I spend a lot of time on the beach, but more as a guest, you know?" I laughed.

He laughed, too. "Exactly. I'm kind of the same way. More like a customer."

"Yeah," I agreed with a giggle. "I'm not sure I'll

make it all the way through the program." Then I sighed, remembering I had swimming on Tuesday night. When I'd been accepted for the Junior Lifeguards program, it was conditional on me taking extra swim lessons each week. I can swim okay, but I'm just not great at it. Bud likes to accept kids based more on attitude and potential because he says he can teach kids to improve their physical skills but not their personalities.

Hayden's smile faded, too, as we reached the pavilion. "Junior Lifeguards won't be easy, that's for sure. But I don't have a lot of other options this summer, so I've got to make this work."

I looked closely at him. There was some sadness around the corners of his mouth and his dark eyes seemed even darker suddenly, which surprised me. He appeared to be the typical preppy summer rich kid who had it all. What could he have to be unhappy about? I wasn't sure if I should press for info or just let it go, but right then something caught my eye so I didn't have to decide.

I turned my head to the right just in time to see

a tiny yellow animal dart around the corner of the pavilion, to the garbage area in the back.

"Did you see that?" I asked, putting my hand on Hayden's shoulder. It was warm and felt strong under the light tee shirt. I think you can tell a lot about people by the way they feel to the touch: skittish, secure, friendly, cold, warm.

Hayden looked at me. "What?"

"Come!" I said, grabbing him by the arm and pulling him toward the back of the beach pavilion.

"Leeny!" Ziggy called from behind.

"Be right back!" I called, waving with my free hand.

"What was it?" asked Hayden.

"I think I just saw a little cat!" I cried. We drew near the edge of the building. "Okay, shh, now. We don't want to scare it," I cautioned.

"It went back here?" Hayden whispered.

I nodded and let go of his arm so we could file through the opening.

We tiptoed around the corner and there it was, sitting next to a giant dumpster, looking up at it hopefully. It was a kitten, teeny tiny, a little yellow striped scamp of a thing, skinny with giant ears. The image of it sitting next to the enormous dumpster reminded me of an inspirational meme, saying something like *"Dream big!"* Instinctively, I reached for my phone but I hesitated, thinking of Bud, and then didn't take it out.

I giggled. "He's so cute!" I whispered.

"Do you think it belongs to someone?" asked Hayden quietly.

"I have no idea. I bet it's hungry. Let's see if Hugo will give us some food and water for it. Come!" I pulled Hayden along with me again. "Stay there, kitty!" I whispered over my shoulder.

There were still kids coming up from the beach but I didn't want to say anything about the kitten. If everyone swarmed back there looking for the kitty it would surely be scared away. I avoided looking at anyone and instead darted straight into the Clam Pot's swinging door. There were a couple of kids waiting on line to pay for ice cream bars and cold drinks.

"Hugo!" I called. He was in the back chopping

lettuce for the next day. He looked up and smiled when he saw us.

"How was it?" he called.

I waved my hand; I didn't want to get into discussing my first day of Junior Lifeguards right now. "It was fine. Listen, do you have any seafood? I want to feed a little kitty we found outside. I think it's a stray."

Hugo put down his knife and wiped his hands on his apron. He came up to the counter, off to the side and beckoned us to join him.

"Hi," he said to Hayden.

"Oh, Hayden, this is my brother Hugo." They shook hands.

Hugo said, "So, what's going on?"

I started from the top. "We just found this tiny kitten hanging out around the back by the dumpster. He's super-skinny and seems like he's looking for food. We think it's a stray. Do you have anything we could feed it?"

Hugo furrowed his brow. "How do you know it doesn't belong to someone else?"

I put my palms in the air. "How would a kitten have gotten this far from home? The nearest house is basically ours and we know no one has a kitten there."

Someone called Hugo away for a minute. When I turned to Hayden, I realized he was looking at me in confusion. "You live around here?" he asked, perplexed.

Oops. "Uh, yeah. Pretty nearby . . ." Now I was trapped because I didn't want to explain the whole my mom's-Samantha Frankel's-maid thing, but I couldn't do my usual thing and imply that my family was rich.

"Wow. Swanky," said Hayden in admiration.

I wanted to tell him the truth but I was too embarrassed. "It's not what you think," was all I could muster. My face burned. With Samantha here full-time for the summer, I had to be more careful in how I presented myself.

Luckily Hugo returned and the moment passed.

Hugo said, "Well, I guess we could feed it a little something. If it's lost, this would be the only place for people to put up signs, so I'll keep my eyes open for that. Hang on."

He went in the back and Hayden and I stood there awkwardly for a second. I hoped the kitten would still be there when we got back.

"Want to go back out and see if it's still there?" I asked.

Hayden looked at me. "Will your brother know where to come?"

I was already walking. "Yup," I said over my shoulder.

As we exited, I looked to see which of my friends were still around. Ziggy was just getting into her mom's Prius. Jenna's bike was gone so that meant she was, too. And I couldn't see Piper because a big SUV had just pulled up to the top of the parking lot at the side closest to me and obscured the rest of my view.

The SUV's windows were tinted and the car was brand-new, with shiny chrome details and fancy rims. That wasn't something you see too much around here. I paused.

"Check *that* out," I said to Hayden, gesturing at the car.

"Wow, swank," he said.

"Hashtag goals," I agreed. Just then every window in the car rolled down and I could see a family inside. Two adults in the front, two little kids in the back.

I was about to turn away when something about the guy driving the car caught me eye. I put my hand on Hayden's arm. "Am I crazy," I whispered. "Or does that guy look just like Indigo Darling?"

"The actor?" asked Hayden, squinting.

It was dim inside the car but it sure looked like him.

"Yeah. You don't think it could be, do you?" I said skeptically.

"Should we go ask him?" chuckled Hayden. "*Hey, pardon me but are you . . . .?*"

I sighed. "It would never be him. What would a famous actor like him be doing here? It's not like this is the Hamptons! But gosh, wouldn't that be cool?" I took another long look and the guy turned and caught me staring. He kind of smiled.

I gasped and spun away. "OMG he just busted me and I totally think it's him. *It's him!* Should we try and get a photo? No one's going to believe we saw him unless we get a photo! I totally worship him. I've seen every one of his movies. I . . . I . . ." I began fanning my face in a panic, just as Hugo walked out with a plastic basket of fish sticks.

"Here we go! One kitty meal, coming right up!"

Then he took a look at me and stopped, and right then the car began backing out of the lot and away from the beach.

"Wait!" I cried weakly. I looked at Hayden. "I didn't get a photo! Should I run after them?"

Hayden laughed. "We don't even know if it was him for sure. I'd just . . ." He looked at the car as it pulled an arc in reverse and then turned to drive away. "Can you take a photo of the car?" He shrugged.

I sagged in disappointment.

"What was that all about?" asked Hugo, confused. "And where's the cat?"

I laid my head on Hugo's shoulder and fake cried. "I think that was just the movie star Indigo Darling in that car! And I blew my chance to get a photo!" I wailed.

"Whaaaat?" Hugo turned as if to look at the car, but of course it was gone. "Really?" He looked to Hayden for confirmation.

Hayden smiled a crooked smile and turned his palms up in the air. "It *might* have been?"

Hugo patted me. "Sorry, sissy. But look at the bright side. It's only Monday. Maybe he'll come back! Now I've got to hurry because it's almost closing time and then I'm due at the theater. Let's go find this cat."

I slumped back to the dumpster area, leading Hugo and Hayden along with me. As we reached the area, I saw the cat dart to hide behind some boxes.

"Here kitty, kitty," I called. Nothing. Maybe he could hear the disappointment in my voice so he was avoiding me.

Hayden made some kissy noises and Hugo did

a little whistle. There was a rustle behind the boxes so we did know he was in there, but the cat did not appear.

We all looked at each other. "It's not like he's tame, so why would he come to us anyway?" said Hayden.

"Because we're nice?" I said hopefully.

"Because we have food," said Hugo confidently. He knelt down and broke up the fried fish sticks with his hands, gasping because it was a little hot. As he broke through the crunchy fried coating, the aroma of fresh fish wafted through the air. Another rustle came from behind the boxes. That kitten had a good nose. Suddenly his little head poked out shyly.

"Hey kitty!" I squealed, but Hugo shushed me.

"He's timid. Here, let's put the food where he can reach it and then we'll back away."

As Hugo moved forward, the cat dived back behind the boxes. Hugo did as he said and we all stood way back by the corner of the building. Slowly, cautiously, the kitten made its way out.

It sniffed at the fish in the basket, tentative. The tip of its yellow tail flicked in the air.

"Come on kitty, I paid good money for that fish," whispered Hugo.

I looked at him. "You *paid* for it?"

Hugo looked at me, all innocent. "Duh. Yeah! Otherwise it would be stealing."

"*Dios mio*," I rolled my eyes. "Saint Hugo. Two fish sticks and he pays for them."

Satisfied that the food was not poisoned, the cat settled in for a good meal, its paws tucked in tightly and its tail swishing behind it.

"Awww!" said Hayden quietly. "You were right! He *was* hungry!"

I nudged him with my elbow. "See that? I'm the cat whisperer," I said.

We laughed.

Suddenly, behind us we could hear Bud's voice calling. "Hayden? Hay-*den*?"

"Oops. I gotta go. Thanks. That was fun—kittens and movie stars."

"Oh. Okay. You're getting a ride from Bud?" I asked. That was odd.

Hayden nodded without elaborating and gave us both a salute. "See you tomorrow!" he called as he jogged backward out of the garbage alley and then turned and ran off.

Hugo and I stood watching the cat eat greedily.

"I hope she doesn't make herself sick," said Hugo.

"She?" I said. "I think it's a boy. I'm calling it Oscar."

Hugo looked at me and laughed. "It's not yours. I'm sure someone will come claim it tomorrow."

"No way. That thing is super-skinny! I bet it hasn't eaten in days. *Pobrecito*. He just needs some TLC. I hope he doesn't get eaten by a coyote out here." Coyotes are actually a real threat here on the Cape. Lots of people didn't even let their cats outdoors anymore, because the coyotes would eat them.

"Don't get any ideas," cautioned Hugo. "No way would Mami let you have that cat at home."

I narrowed my eyes and batted them at him. "Don't be so sure, mister."

"Hello? The Frankels? Alright, I'm out. Gotta close the shop," said Hugo, turning away.

"Thanks for the fish," I said.

"Later," called Hugo over his shoulder.

"See you at home," I called. *"With my new kitty!"* I added in a whisper. "Right, Oscar?" Since I knew Bud was gone, I slid my phone out of my bag and snapped a pic of the kitty. I wasn't planning on posting it because I didn't want everyone to come storming around looking for him, even my best friends.

Posting a photo of Indigo Darling would have been a different story.

Maintenance

My parents let me sleep a little bit late the next day, which got me off to a great start. Even though I had to meet Martin again at ten for my tutoring, I had time to spare.

Tuesdays are always maintenance days for me, along with Saturdays. It's when I do all my beauty regimens and update all my social media accounts. I get all my regimens off the internet, and most of the stuff I use is all natural and homemade. Today I did a hydrating mask on my face with olive oil, then I took a long shower and exfoliated with sea salt. Now that I'm thirteen my mami is finally allowing me to shave my legs (thank goodness), so I did that and afterward I smoothed body oil all over my skin. It wasn't worth spending any time on my hair, since I knew it would be wet by day's end, but a future star does have to take great care of her skin as an investment.

Up in the big house, Mrs. Frankel has a skirted dressing table with one of those mirrors with the light bulbs all around it, like a real star would have in a theater dressing room. In the master bathroom, she has a magnifying mirror to see her skin up close, and a whole kit of makeup and skin care products all neatly arrayed on the dressing table, even though she's hardly ever here. Since she's a newscaster and on the air all the time, she probably has to wear a lot of makeup, even though she's usually out in the field on location. I'm sure she has an incredible skin care regimen. I've Googled pictures of her from when she was starting out as a model in London (by way of Somalia), and even though that was twenty years ago, she looks the exact same now.

Sometimes in the winter, when my mom is downstairs cleaning, I climb the stairs to the Frankels' master bedroom and sit at the dressing table and pretend I am already a star. Looking in the magnifying mirror is weirdly addictive. You wouldn't believe what you can see that close. I swear that an hour has gone by sometimes with me just squeezing and poking and checking myself from different angles.

When I'm famous, I'll have a really fancy bedroom, too. The whole vintage movie star look appeals to me: my room will be all cream and pink and gold and I'll wear a pink silk bathrobe cinched tight, with those high-heeled slides with marabou feathers on them, and my hair up in a stretchy pink terrycloth turban. But for now, I have to make do with a bathroom I share with Hugo that is cramped and has no counter space and very little room for me to store my things. Lots of stars start out this way, or so I've read.

This morning, after my bathing ritual, I moved on to career maintenance. I have my own YouTube channel, and besides videos of me singing, I like to post vlogs about movies I've seen (I try to do one every other week). Another thing I like to vlog about is Movie Recasts, where I'll describe a recast of a film with actors I would like to see in the roles (sometimes it's an update or a remake of a classic movie, with modern actors; other times it's just who I would prefer to see in a role of a new movie) and often I'll put myself in an appropriate starring role, with real actors I'm dying to work with in the other roles.

Today I finished up by posting a picture of Indigo Darling to my Pinterest board, then it was time to organize my lifeguarding gear, pack up my tutoring stuff and head out to start my day.

Okay, I still don't like math, but today Martin pointed out that I'll need math skills later in life to make sure my manager isn't cheating me out of my money (it happens all the time in Hollywood). For today, Martin had even put together some sample problems for me that were about box office gross and film budgets and other useful things.

"Did you hear anything about any movie stars being around here this summer?" I asked.

Martin tipped his head. "Hmm, no. Not yet anyway. Like who?"

I shrugged casually. "Oh, I just saw someone last night at Lookout beach who looked so much like Indigo Darling."

"Really? Wow. I saw him in summer stock in Williamstown one time. He is incredible on-stage . . ." raved Martin.

"He's incredible *everywhere!*" I agreed. "I've got to do some digging on social media and see if I can find out if anyone's posted about him being here yet."

"Just another use for social media," said Martin darkly, teasing me.

"And there are many!" I teased back.

"Just remember, if you feel good about your-self, you don't need outside validation. That's my sermon for today."

"Oh, Martin. Don't be such a blue-haired coder," I joked.

After working with Martin, I popped my head in to the library's Children's Room to say hi to Janet and Harry Potter the cat, and then left to grab a smoothie for lunch before lifeguards. Town was kind of quiet, it being so early in the season, but people were already starting to gear up for the tourists' arrival. Clothing stores had mannequins out front, dressed in bright colors and snappy prints. The Vineyard Vines store had the console of a real Hinckley boat in the window, and the mannequins all had on cute navy and white outfits with American flags in their hands. The bookstore had a cart out front with used "beach read" paperbacks for the taking. The ice cream store was already open for the day and the smell of their homemade waffle cones drifted on the breeze, tantalizing me with the aroma of caramelizing sugar.

I took my Lean Green Protein shake to a bench

in the park and sat in the shade for a few minutes to drink it. There were some little kids playing on the slide and their moms were seated on a bench near me, chatting and drinking their coffee. I watched the kids and it reminded me of when I was younger and played here, which seems like five minutes ago and also a lifetime ago.

Suddenly my ears pricked up.

"It's like Hollywood on the Sound!" one of the moms was saying.

"I know! It's so exciting! Our own little brush with fame!"

I snuck a peek at them. What were they talking about? I willed them to say more so I could figure it out.

"Did you see *Alarming* when it was in theaters?"

"Oh, yes! I wouldn't have missed it! He was so dreamy in that film!"

"I know. He looks just as good in real life, I must say. I hear that isn't usually the case with stars."

Alarming was a movie starring Indigo Darling. Could it be that they were talking about him?

"His wife is really pretty, too. And they were very down to earth, just walking along Main Street, holding hands, with the kids running ahead. So cute!"

Okay, wait a minute. *Main Street?* Like, *our* Main Street?

"Where are they staying?" asked one of the mothers.

"I heard someone say they rented a house for the week. Just something modest, not even on the water."

The mothers nodded their approval. I was now blatantly staring at them and obviously eavesdropping. I had to say something.

"Excuse me, I'm sorry to be listening in . . ."

The mothers laughed, and waved off my apology. "We're not exactly having a meeting of the minds," joked one of them.

". . . .so were you just saying that Indigo Darling is in town?" I continued.

The two ladies beamed at sharing the news.

"Yes!" said one of them, nodding in excitement.

"And I saw him last night in town!" added the other with a grin.

"*Here?*" I cried.

"Uh-huh! Right over there, in fact!" she pointed to the other side of the street where most of the stores were.

"Oh my gosh! I thought I saw him at Lookout yesterday, but then I just couldn't believe it was really him! OMG! And it was!!!" My stomach did a flip-flop and goosebumps tingled up my arms. I'd seen a real, live star! "Did you get a photo?" I asked eagerly.

"No, I didn't even think of it," said one of the moms.

"I'm sure there will be another chance. Some-one said he's here for a week while he's on break from filming his new movie."

I was confused. "But why would he pick here? I mean, why not Osterville or P-Town or something more fancy? Or even one of the islands? The Vine-yard seems to be a major star haven." (I know this from *People* magazine online and am always begging to be allowed to take the ferry over to Martha's Vineyard for the day and go celeb-spotting, but my parents never have time to take me in the summer and they won't let me go alone because 'it's too far at your age!').

One of the ladies tipped her head thoughtfully. "I think he's from around here, right?"

"What? Seriously? I'd never heard that!" How had I missed that important fact?

"Mmm-hmm," agreed the other lady. "I read that somewhere one time. That he lived here for a bit when he was a boy. I think he even went to school here for a while."

I couldn't believe it! "What? That is so cool! I need to search that."

I opened up my browser on my phone and typed in his name and the Wikipedia entry came up first. As I scrolled down to "early life," the ladies continued talking about all the movies they'd loved him in and how they've always heard that he's a good guy in real life.

"Don't you just love it when celebrities are nice?" said one.

"Totally," agreed the other.

I made a mental note to always be nice to people once I'm famous.

Quickly I scanned the biographical facts and sure enough, it showed that he had lived on the Cape from the ages of eight to thirteen, before his mother moved them to join family in California.

"Huh! You're right! He *did* live here as a kid! He went to Chatham Elementary!" Well, that was certainly satisfying news. If someone as big as him came from here, then maybe I do have a shot at the big time!

The time on my phone caught my eye and I realized I needed to go. I said goodbye to the ladies and thanked them for sharing their intel.

"Good luck! I hope you spot him!" said one of them, as I threw away my smoothie cup and wheeled my bike out to the street.

"Thanks! You, too. And I hope we all get photos next time." I smiled and waved and then pedaled away, my heart leaping in hope at every corner. Maybe I'd see him again, if I just looked carefully enough at every black SUV that passed me by.

Today I arrived at the beach a tiny bit earlier than yesterday. Whether it was intentional or not, I couldn't say, but it felt good being there and ready by twelve forty-five. I parked my bike in the rack and locked it, and I was thinking of joining the small knot of kids down on the sand, but thought instead I'd quickly see if Oscar the kitty was around.

I crossed the rough planks of the pavilion, my flip-flops slapping softly against the soles of my feet. At the far end, I rounded the corner to enter the little alley, and bumped right into . . . Samantha and Hayden.

"Um . . . Hey?" I said. I was confused and caught off guard. My face burned.

"Hi!" said Hayden, a little too brightly, if you ask me. He blushed a little, too.

Samantha just looked vaguely in my direction

and smiled her closed-lip smile, which made her look super-smug. Through my buzz of annoyance I made a mental note to practice the look later in the mirror; it would be quite handy for portraying unlikeable characters.

"Hi," I said flatly. I knew I had no claim to this space or to the kitten, but I was annoyed to see them there together, and to have to interact with Samantha at all. *Thank goodness I didn't tell Hayden about my living arrangements yesterday,* was all I could think.

There was an awkward silence, then, "We just found the most darling kitten!" Samantha said in her swanky accent.

Found? Seriously? Of all the nerve! And this is the first thing she can say to me all summer?

I looked at Hayden and I'm sure confusion and hurt were written all over my face, but I wasn't about to admit anything out loud, and he just looked away.

"Really," I said coolly, more a statement than a question. It took all of my self-control not to scream

at Hayden for the betrayal. Meryl Streep couldn't have done it any better.

"Hey, I hope you don't mind," said Hayden, caving as he met my eye finally. "I just wanted to check on him, and I brought Samantha since she said she loved cats."

Quickly I turned to look at her. "You do?" I spoke without meaning to, but I was surprised to have anything in common with one of the Frankel girls.

"Oh yes, I adore them! They start out so cute and sweet and playful, and when they grow up they become elegant and wise and aloof. It's an amazing transition!" It was the most I'd ever heard her say.

I furrowed my brow. "Wait, do you have a cat?" I'd never heard of the Frankels having any pets, and Samantha was quickly shaking her head.

"No. We travel too much for us to have one, and my mum thinks it cruel to drag animals with you on jets and into hotels and whatnot."

"Oh!" I said, nodding in agreement as if that might also be a reasonable consideration for me. It was the first time I'd ever heard *that* excuse for a family not getting a pet.

"Hey, he's still here!" cried Hayden, unable to contain his excitement.

"He is?" I crept in and spotted the kitten immediately. He saw me and froze, but he didn't run away this time.

"Remember me?" I whispered, squatting down to his level so as not to intimidate him.

Oscar looked me over and then went back to what he was doing, which was playing with a wire baggie tie. He was lifting it between his two front paws and standing on his hind legs as he tried to manipulate it. Then it dropped and he hopped around trying to pick it back up again. It was super cute to watch him play. I giggled. I was psyched he felt secure enough with me to not run away this time.

Hayden was behind me and whispered, "Isn't he so funny?"

I had to smile. "Yes! He is such a cutie!"

"Hey, Spot!" called Samantha from behind me.

It startled the cat and he took off like a streak to hide behind the dumpster.

I stood up. "His name is Oscar," I said, brushing the sand from my fingertips.

"We should get him more food," said Hayden. "He's got to maintain his weight so he can keep growing."

I waited for Hayden to tell Samantha she'd scared him off, but he didn't. I couldn't exactly reprimand her, given my position. I sighed. It was time for bear crawls anyway.

"I'll come by later and give him some more fish from the Clam Pot," I said. "I can pay for it today; I brought money."

"You're buying him food from the snack bar?" laughed Samantha. "Why don't you just catch him and bring him home?"

I looked at her. Could she really think life was that easy?

"We can't have a cat," I said coldly. I wasn't about to list my family's reasons why, considering reason number one was her family! I turned on my heel and stalked off so they wouldn't see the tears of shame pricking at my eyes.

The warm-ups were hideous again (I wore shorts over my suit this time, though, to avoid the public wedgie-a-thon), and I was in a foul mood, but when it came time for the jog, Bud made me laugh.

"We are the junior lifeguards, the mighty junior lifeguards . . ." he began, as he took off running with us all behind him. "Wait, that doesn't sound right. How does this go again? Selena, get up here!"

I had to laugh in spite of my grumpiness. I jogged up to join him and gave him a fake punch in the arm. "No, Bud. You've got it all wrong! Come on!" I joked. "It goes, *We are the lifeguards, the mighty, mighty lifeguards . . . .*"

"Right!" He joined in singing with me.

After a bit we took requests, and the jog passed quickly.

"Selena, You are our official music director for

the Junior Lifeguards program, okay?" Bud said at the end.

I looked down modestly, not wanting to meet anyone's eyes. But if I'd had to guess, Ziggy and Piper would have been proudly beaming at me, while Jenna scowled and Samantha stared out to sea.

After, Bud read the assignments from his clipboard. As luck would have it, Jenna and I were put together for the afternoon. I waited to hear if anyone else was coming but it was just us two, with Daniel (who was a silent and geeky college-aged guard), to be stationed at Sea Spray, the ocean beach.

Today was a plum assignment and if I was more ambitious about lifeguarding, I would have been flattered and excited to be given such a serious job. Sea Spray Beach was not for hacks and Daniel was not there to tell stories about toddlers pooping in the sand, like Jessie had yesterday. *Dios mio*, today would be work . . . in more ways than one. Even though I wasn't getting along with Jenna, I was so relieved that I wasn't paired with Samantha. Though she'd spoken to me in the privacy of the garbage area, she hadn't uttered another word to me in our group warm up. We were back to our unspoken agreement of ignoring each other, which was just fine with me.

Jenna walked ahead of me to grab her stuff. I jogged along to catch up and she was already riding by the time I got to my bike. She was acting like she was really mad at me. I know my singing was annoying her, but it wasn't like I was being directly mean to her. What the heck? There was no way to talk on the ride because we had to go single file on a busy street.

At Sea Spray, Jenna quickly locked her bike and walked down onto the sand; I trotted along behind her trying to catch up.

Daniel was patrolling the shore and said hello shyly when we reached him. He explained some of the quirks of this particular beach, like where the riptides usually formed due to the little island spit offshore, and how we need to keep kids off the slippery rocks of the jetty. Like yesterday, the beach was not busy, so he asked us to patrol the water's edge for a bit and do some beach maintenance, picking up any garbage we saw and then raking the seaweed into piles for removal.

I grabbed the trash bag he offered us for the garbage collection, and Jenna and I set out. I wanted to talk to Jenna but I wasn't sure how to start. She was supposed to be one of my best friends but now I felt as awkward around her as I did around Samantha Frankel.

"Hey look at these awesome shells!" I said, picking up some of the gold jingle shells I'd loved since I was little. Hugo and I had always called them *"abuela's aretes,"* which means 'grandma's earrings' in Spanish, since they reminded us of the wild earrings our grandmother used to wear to parties and weddings back in Ecuador. "I should collect these an put them in a jar on my dresser. I just don't have anywhere to carry them!" I patted my bathing suit like I was looking for pockets, but this didn't elicit even a smile from Jenna.

Jenna stooped to pick up a beer bottle cap and

a slice of battered blue plastic, and put them in the garbage bag.

"Hello! Earth to Jen!" I joked. She glanced at me but almost didn't seem to see me. "Do I have to be a piece of trash for you to notice me?" I joked, putting my face under hers to look up at her.

Jenna stopped her walk and stood still in the sand. She looked mad.

"What's the matter?" I asked. Of course, I really knew why she was mad, but I wanted to hear her say it. I braced myself for a diatribe about being a suck-up to Bud.

But instead, Jenna took a deep breath and growled, "What's the matter is, you were holding hands with Hayden Jones at the beach yesterday!"

Whaaaaat?

Finding a Rhythm

"Jenna, I have no idea what you're talking about! Holding hands? When?"

Jenna resumed her beach walk, but she was storming along now. I jogged to keep up.

Jenna laughed like a little bark. "Ha! As if you don't know!"

I was truly confused. "I don't even . . . I really . . ."

Jenna stopped again. "Look, I know you're all Ms. Touchy Feely, always putting your hands on people and all Latina and lovey-dovey. And now you're going after Hayden with your lovey ways!"

She began stalking up the beach and I darted again to keep up.

"What do you mean? When was I touchy feely with Hayden?" I sidestepped along to face her and keep up at the same time.

"See, you don't even remember! It doesn't even *mean* anything to you. But it does to other people!" Jenna spun to face me. "When you grabbed Hayden yesterday after training, and dragged him up somewhere to hide behind the pavilion and, and . . . kiss or something! Ugh! You had your hands all over him! It was disgusting! You can't stop your compulsive flirting. First it's Hayden, then it's Bud, next I'm sure it will be poor nerdy Daniel for goodness' sake!"

I was truly shocked. This time, as Jenna marched off down the beach, I just stood there, flabbergasted. What on earth was she talking about? I reviewed yesterday, when Hayden and I had gone up to see where the kitten had run. Was I holding his hand? Now that I thought about it, I remembered grabbing his arm, and how it was warm and strong. But I hadn't held his hand. And I certainly wasn't 'flirting' with Bud. Gross! Now I was mad, too!

I chased Jenna up the beach.

"You are just making this stuff up, Jenna! I pulled Hayden by the arm to see a kitten yesterday. We weren't *holding hands*! And even if we were, it's not like he has a girlfriend! As for flirting with Bud? That is disgusting. He's, like, a grandpa! I was so bored with all that exercising that I had to do something to keep myself amused, so I sang. I wasn't expecting him to let me keep doing it, never mind join me! You are way out of line accusing me like that!"

Jenna looked like she was going to cry, which is something she almost never does. I saw her take a deep breath and steel herself and will the tears away. "Look, I don't own anyone. I don't have any claim to anyone. I just find it annoying that your automatic default setting with any male of the species is to flirt."

"I don't see it that way. It's not intentional. It's just how I am!"

Jenna stared at me for a long time. I was innocent and I wore it openly on my face. If we were in a movie, this would be where the sun would break through clouds and my co-star would see me for the good person I was. In fact, if we were in a movie right now, a kid would start drowning and I would save them and then Jenna would fall all over herself to apologize to me for thinking I was a bad person, when I was clearly a hero.

Quickly, I scanned the water to see if there was anyone I could save, but all I saw was a seagull, bobbing lazily in the ruffled water. I looked back at Jenna.

She sighed deeply. "You really don't see it, do you?"

"See what?" I pleaded.

"How you are with males," she said.

I shrugged. "I'm just nice to them. I like them." I said. What more could I add?

There was a pause, and then, "Oh, whatever," said Jenna. "Forget it, okay? I'm sorry. I'm overreacting."

"Okay, I'm sorry, too. *Amigas?*" I said with a smile.

Jenna smiled but it was kind of a Samantha smile. No teeth. *"Amigas,"* she agreed.

So Jenna liked Hayden. I had guessed as much during try-outs, but I thought they were just friends. Should I back off just because she was interested in him? But what if I was interested in him, too? He's a free agent. It's a free country. I didn't want to compete with Jenna for the role of "Hayden's Girlfriend," (we might also be competing with Samantha Frankel, too, from what I'd seen today), but who was she to lay claim to him? Maybe he liked me better.

The afternoon passed slowly, and it wound up with Daniel and I down by the water, chatting, and Jenna up in the chair, scouting. She and I had patrolled for a while but honestly there was hardly anyone on the beach (thank goodness—another day without me having to try to save someone with my mediocre swimming skills) and all three of us were bored and restless. Daniel taught us a guarding technique where you section the ocean into quadrants and watch them in rotation, so Jenna asked if she could sit up high to practice and Daniel agreed.

Down on the sand, I was happy for new company. Jenna—despite agreeing we were friends again—had not been chatty today and guarding together had been a strain. We were both avoiding conversational minefields, like the topics of Samantha and of Hayden. It wasn't like Daniel was co-star material, but at least he was someone to talk to who would make uncomplicated conversation with me.

"What's your favorite movie?" I asked him, as we strolled. This is always my favorite opening question and it's a good test of someone's personality or at least interests. I like to hone my skills of observation by making a private prediction before they answer; I'm pretty good at it. I'm guessing Daniel goes with something Sci Fi: either super-hero or outer space,

Daniel squinted at the sky for a minute. "Mmm. Anything *Star Wars*, I guess."

Bingo!

I nodded in encouragement. "Old or new ones better?"

"I guess old," he said, warming to the topic. "I mean, they're classic, they're kind of the origin of the franchise, even though it's not the origin story, you know? And they're so exciting and the effects are surprisingly good . . . ."

"I agree. I prefer the old ones, too." I wasn't much of one for special effects—give me a RomCom (romantic comedy) any day—but no one can top the box office power of *Star Wars*. It's epic, and you just have to admire it.

"Have you seen any good movies lately?" asked Daniel.

"Oh, nothing good. The movies are so expensive that it really has to be a biggie for me to see it in theaters rather than stream it or check a DVD out of the library."

"Do you know who Indigo Darling is?" said Daniel, taking me completely by surprise.

I laughed. "Of course! And did you hear . . ."

Daniel smiled and nodded his head. "I know! He's here in town! I saw him at Vinny's Pizza last night with his family."

I grabbed his arm and jumped up and down. "You did not!"

Daniel was laughing now. I quickly thought of Jenna and dropped his arm like a hot potato, not daring to sneak a peek at the lifeguard stand. I only hoped we weren't in the quadrant she was watching at the moment.

"This is driving me crazy. It's such a small town and I keep missing him! I mean, he was up at Lookout yesterday but I wasn't sure it was really him until the last minute. And then it was too late to get a photo. Ugh! I just know I'll never see him. It's so unfair! Did you get a photo?"

But Daniel shook his head no. What was wrong with people? Didn't they want to prove to their friends that they'd seen a celebrity? Didn't they want something to post on Instagram later?

"But I heard he's staying on Shepherd's Path," offered Daniel. "Maybe you could ride your bike by . . . ?"

"Like, stalk him?" I joked, raising my eyebrows with an evil grin.

Daniel shrugged. "When you put it that way . . ."

I sighed. "I'll give it a few more days. If I don't see him by Friday, it's time for desperate measures." I mimed the hand gestures of an evil wizard, putting my palms together and wiggling my fingertips greedily. *Mwwwaaa-ha-ha-ha!*" I gave a villainous laugh and rubbed my palms together briskly.

"Uh-oh!" teased Daniel. "We never had this conversation!"

I gave him a playful smack on the arm. "If I get busted for stalking, I'll say you were the mastermind behind the whole thing. That you loved him in *Star Wars* and insisted I get you his photo!"

"But he wasn't in *Star Wars!*" protested Daniel in confusion.

"And *that's* how they'll know you're really crazy!" I said in a sinister tone.

Oscar the kitten came right out when I called him at the end of the day today. I had the fish sticks ready to go and it was like he was expecting me. This time, I didn't tell anyone I was going in to see him. I wanted to keep him to myself.

I broke up the fish and set it out and sat to the side to watch him eat it (I'd brought three pieces this time—and paid for it, too). Oscar was such a delicate eater—it was really cute. He'd lift a big piece of fish in his teeth and take a tiny bite of it, and the rest of it would drop back in the bowl, but he would kind of panic that he'd dropped it, so he'd move to the side to try again, but he'd realize he had gotten some in his mouth, so he'd chew it really quickly, then start all over again. I was giggling quietly watching him.

Suddenly I sensed someone nearby and I looked up. It was Samantha.

"Hey," she whispered. "How's the little guy?" She sat down quietly next to me.

"Cute," I said flatly. I was confused by Samantha's behavior—she was hot and cold. Were we supposed to speak, or not? Did we only speak in private, but not in the group? Did she not want to be seen associating with the help? She seemed to be following a rule book I hadn't seen.

Samantha was very placid, though, just watching Oscar, so I followed her lead and said nothing. Finally she said, "Gosh, I really wish I could have one of these little critters. Every holiday I beg for one, and every year my mum says no."

It was hard for me to picture Samantha Frankel not getting everything she wanted. I didn't know what to say and the minute stretched on uncomfortably, until finally I asked, "Couldn't someone take care of a cat for you at home?" As soon as the words were out of my mouth I realized I'd just put us both in an awkward position.

But Samantha handled it well.

"It wouldn't be right for me to get a cat and then just have someone look after it for me. It wouldn't be fair to the kitty. It needs someone to love it as their own."

I knew what she meant so I just nodded.

"Why can't you have him?" she asked.

I sighed. How to explain this? "Well . . . my mother feels . . . it's just . . . you see . . ." I paused for a second. "It's not really our place to have a pet on the property," I finished all in a rush. I wanted this conversation to be over. I wanted Samantha to leave and let me be here alone with Oscar.

Samantha nodded.

After a second I realized that she wasn't going to comment, but she also wasn't going anywhere.

I broke the silence next. "I might get him some real cat food to bring down here, though. I mean, if I'm going to keep feeding him, it's probably not so good for his cholesterol if he keeps eating fried fish."

Samantha looked at me. "You'd make a good kitty mama," she said.

"Hashtag goals!" I said wryly, letting some of my personality creep out.

"It *is* a goal of mine!" she actually laughed. "Sadly enough. I don't have many."

"I have tons," I said, ticking them off on my finger. "Get a starring role in a movie or TV show, have a song on the Top 40, set a record for the most likes ever on YouTube, get a photo with a major movie star, pass math, get a cat . . ." Ugh. I was so nervous I was rambling. I closed my mouth.

Samantha's eyes were wide. "Wow! You *are* motivated! I feel like such a slacker compared to you!"

I looked at her sideways. "My parents are big on us working hard at everything."

"You say that like it's a bad thing," she said lightly, standing up and brushing the sand off her hands.

"Trust me, it's not a good thing," I said. "My parents are taskmasters."

"At least they pay attention to you," said Samantha.

"Um . . ." I wasn't sure how to respond.

"Gotta dash!" Samantha said all of a sudden, fake-brightly, and she left.

Our intimate little bubble had popped and now I *really* had no idea how I was supposed to interact with Samantha the next time I saw her. That chat in the alley had been more like confession than friendship. At least no one was around to see it, so I could pretend it never happened.

And now, drumroll please . . . the moment I'd been dreading for weeks had finally arrived. If my life were a movie, it would have just done a jump cut from me laughing on the beach with a cute boy, the wind tousling my wavy hair, to me standing miserably in a chilly indoor pool with my wet hair plastered to the sides of my head, surrounded by nerds.

So here I was in the pool at the YMCA with Bud Slater, and two other Junior Lifeguard kids, both slightly younger than I am, both boys, and we were about to have our free weekly swim lesson. Good times. *Not!*

Bud had on a wet suit top that made me jealous. The pool wasn't freezing but it wasn't bathwater either, and we were just standing there inhaling the awful chlorine fumes. He was showing us a breathing rhythm, and pretty soon he was going to send us off to try it across the shallow end of the pool with kickboards (so humiliating!), but he seemed distracted and kept looking at the door. Every time he looked, I looked. What or who were we waiting for, I wondered.

"Alright, here are your kickboards," Bud said finally, like he was giving us something we'd really been looking forward to. "Come on down to the shallow end and line up against the wall."

"Sounds like we're going to be executed," I muttered, but no one heard me, or at least no one laughed.

When Bud gave us the command to "Go!" we took off, each of us with both hands holding a kickboard, arms outstretched, kicking and turning our heads to breathe at the right moment.

Except for the fact that I felt like a toddler, for the first few kicks everything went well. My first breath was fine, and my second. But on my third breath, I caught a drop of water in my throat and began to sputter. I was sure I was going to drown. I stopped and put my feet on the bottom of the pool so I could stand up, gasping.

"Okay, Selena?" Bud was at my side immediately.

I coughed again and cleared my throat. The other two kids seemed to be doing fine. This was so embarrassing. "I think so," I croaked.

Bud nodded. "Just try again. I'm right here. Nothing's going to happen to you."

Right, I thought. *I'm the one who's going to be saving people and I can't even save myself.*

I made it five breaths this time before I began to sputter. I stood and choked and Bud came over.

"Maybe see if it happens again, if you can keep going, or at least, don't stand. Get used to treading water while you get back on track. Can you do that?" he asked kindly. Private Lesson Bud was warmer and fuzzier than Head of Lifeguards Bud. That was a silver lining. If he'd been strict or mean I totally would have left.

Meanwhile the other two kids were cruising back and forth. This would probably be their only session, I thought morosely.

I took a deep breath again and tried to settle down.

"Hey!" said Bud. "Here's an idea. Do what you do with the jogging at lifeguard training. Sing a song in your head. Like running, it helps if you have something to keep time to. It can distract you a little, too."

I tipped my head to the side and thought. "Okay," I said. I splashed my hands on the surface of the water. "Got it! *Boom Boom Pow* by the Black Eyed Peas!"

Bud grinned. "Great! Try again!"

This time, it worked! I sang along in my head and somehow the song kept me kicking and breathing on schedule and I didn't suck in any drops, or maybe just one but it didn't end up bothering me as much and I didn't stop. I imagined myself in a movie montage, with a series of quick scenes set to great music like I was picturing during beach warm-ups yesterday. I do love a good montage! Here's Selena, drowning in the pool and getting lifted out by Bud; here's Selena, struggling with bear crawls and falling down on the sand; here's Selena, unable to lift a CPR dummy. But then: here's Selena working hard and Bud blowing whistles in her face while she runs in place; and here's Selena in the pool spluttering and trying again and again; and here's Selena, working with the other guards to lift and carry stuff. And finally, here's Selena, whipping through the bear crawls on the beach and leaving the others in the dust with a laugh, and here's Selena, diving into the ocean and swimming straight out with beautiful strokes and breaths to save a kid from drowning, and here's Indigo Darling on the beach, clapping for Selena . . .

While enjoying my fantasy montage, I kicked back and forth three times without stopping, just turning around when my board bumped the side of the pool. And when I finally finished, I popped up in victory with my fists in the air like Rocky the prizefighter and found myself face to feet with Hayden Jones.

A Sinking Feeling

"Hayden?" I looked up at him in shock and he looked down at me, equally surprised to see me there.

"Hayden!" yelled Bud from across the pool. "Where have you been?"

Hayden tore his eyes away and walked briskly over to Bud.

"Sorry, sir. My bicycle tires needed air and I couldn't find the pump."

Bud sighed in exasperation. "You're twenty minutes late! It doesn't take twenty minutes to find a bicycle pump and pump the tires. I knew I should have made you come in the truck with me."

Hayden said nothing.

"Hop in," said Bud.

Hayden peeled off his tee shirt and jumped into the pool. What on earth was he doing here? Was he going to be Bud's assistant teacher? How embarrassing! Ugh. I was going to have to figure out a way to get out of these lessons, I realized. Like, make up a commitment. Something! I could not have Hayden Jones seeing what a bad swimmer I was!

"All right, everyone over here!" called Bud.

The other kids and I crossed the pool to him and Hayden.

"Next, we're going to work on our kicks," said Bud. "I see you all kicking but the kicks are not effective enough; they're not giving you any power. You want your kicks to look like this . . ." He clutched the side of the wall and kicked vigorously, sending a plume of water way up into the air like Old Faithful. "Okay? Not like this!" and he plunked his feet, alternating one and then the other, in listless kicks that barely raised a splash.

"Could everyone please try that?"

The two younger kids grabbed the wall and did as they were told. Hayden and I eyed each other. I didn't want him to see my sad, plunky kicks, and I guess he was waiting to evaluate me so he could see how he could help. But I wasn't about to give him the opportunity! I folded my arms and stood there, waiting.

"Let's go, you two! It's not a staring contest!" cried Bud.

Hayden sighed and grabbed the wall and began to kick. Wait, what? Why was he doing that? Just to make me feel worse about my skills? His kicks looked good. But mine would be better!

I grabbed the wall and kicked like heck until I was breathless with the effort. This was all starting to remind me of *G.I Jane*, that old movie with Demi Moore, where she trains to be a Navy SEAL. I could play that role in the remake . . . but I'd hate to get a crew cut. Hmmm. Well, maybe if they paid me enough . . .

"Great, Selena!" called Bud from the middle of the pool. "Henry, Lyon, a little stronger please— you're sinking! And Hayden, you can do better than that!"

It was weird that Bud was criticizing his assistant. Maybe it was another motivational tactic of his, like 'we're all equal out here in the water' or something.

I did another vigorous round of kicking and found myself too breathless to go on. I left my feet drift down to the bottom of the pool and squatted, keeping my shoulders under the water to stay warm. I snuck a glance at Hayden and saw that he seemed to be struggling a little, which was weird.

Bud was at his side. "Stretch out your arms a bit; give yourself some room. You might want to put your face in the water to make it a little easier. I know, I know. But I'm right here. Nothing's going to happen. I've got you."

Okay, *whaaaaat*?

Why was Bud acting like Hayden couldn't swim?

I thought back to tryouts and to the couple of times we'd been on the beach together so far. Had I seen Hayden swim? Hmm. Come to think of it, no. Could it be . . . ? I couldn't fathom that a big, sporty-looking, preppy kid like Hayden Jones would not know how to swim. Wasn't he, like, born being able to swim? Weren't all rich, preppy kids? It just didn't add up. But there it was.

If Hayden couldn't swim, the last thing I wanted was to embarrass him by watching him try. I clasped the wall again, dropped my face in the water, and practiced kicking and breathing at the same time until Bud grabbed my foot to get my attention.

We had one more assignment before the end of the session, which was to swim the perimeter of the pool, varying our strokes, for a timed six minutes. At this point, I was basically ignoring Hayden, for both of our sakes. I had decided to pretend he wasn't even here, just to preserve both of our dignity.

I began my swim with the breaststroke for a few laps, then switched to the backstroke, which I love because it reminds me of the glamorous movie stars from the 1940s, in their waterproof lipstick and their bathing caps. Not that I am anywhere near as good a swimmer, just that I need my inspo wherever I can get it. I wished someone could snap a glamorous photo of me right now to post. *#estherwilliams!*

Suddenly, Bud was above me at the side of the pool. "Let's see some freestyle before you finish, Miss Diaz, please."

I sighed heavily and flopped onto my stomach. Even though it moves me through the water faster than anything else, freestyle is my least favorite stroke. I hate the breathing and I hate not being able to see where I'm going.

I started in the shallow end and I was okay at first, maybe because I knew the bottom of the pool was right there if I needed it. But by the time I got to the deep end, where the water was over my head, my energy was flagging and my coordination was off. I tried singing along in my head, and picturing my victorious montage from before, but I was too tired and distracted. I started to sputter and then I took in a big breath of water and began to really panic. I flailed around and suddenly felt strong arms lifting me out of the water and on to the side of the pool.

I dashed the water from my eyes and gasped to regain my breath. Bud was there. "Are you okay?" he asked gravely.

I nodded and hacked through another coughing fit. Bud patted me firmly on the back, his mouth a grim line. "I shouldn't have pushed you at the end," he said. "You'd just done so well so far, I thought you could handle it. You just got tired."

Down at the shallow end I saw that Hayden was taking advantage of Bud's preoccupation by stopping and standing every few feet as he swam. Without turning his head, Bud called, "No stopping, Hayden! Keep those feet off the bottom!"

I spun my head to look at him, wide-eyed. How had he known? But Bud winked. "Lucky guess. Was I right?"

I smiled but I didn't give anything away.

"Look, you're almost there," said Bud. "You just need to stay calm, practice your timing and pacing, and improve your conditioning. A few more sessions here, training every day, we'll have you up and running in no time. And Selena, one word: *confidence*. Okay?"

He stood and blew his whistle. "That's it for to-night, kids! Hit the showers!"

Hayden gratefully strode through the shallow end to the stairs to climb out of the water.

"Not you, Jones!" said Bud. "Back in the water. You've got some lost time to make up for."

I shot a sympathetic look to Hayden but I wasn't sure if he'd noticed and I didn't want to hang around and have him think I was watching him.

"Thanks, Mr. Slater," I said, as I went to grab my towel and leave.

"Nice job, Miss Diaz. You're gonna be a star, don't worry!" said Bud with a grin.

I smiled, hoping he was right in more ways than one, and left without a backward glance.

After dinner that night, I begged my parents to let me bring home Oscar the kitty to live with us. My mother was reading some huge statistics textbook and she stuck her finger in the book to mark her place while she listened to me.

"Please, Mami. I know Samantha wants a cat, too! It can be like her cat and mine that we share!"

My mother scoffed at the idea, actually making a little choking sound in the back of her throat. "Selena, please. No cats on the property. No, *mi amor*. When you are grown up and have your own house, you can get as many cats as you like. But not here."

I tried to play on my dad's sympathy. "Papi, please! I'm doing everything you want this summer. The lifeguards, the tutoring, the swim lessons, the job at the library. Can't I have something *I* want for a change?"

Did I mention my dad is not one for guilt trips? They only make him annoyed.

"Selena, that sounds like a very happy summer to me. Not too many days ago we were talking about sending you to summer school for the whole summer." He snapped open his laptop as if to say, *Case closed.*

Not too many days ago, I *was talking about going to a sleepaway acting camp in Michigan,* I wanted to say. But I didn't. The thing with parents is, you have to know when you can push and when you can't.

I left them and went to my room to sulk.

Upstairs, I was surprised to see I had a message from Jenna. She must have felt bad about how she'd behaved today, because it said:

Bunch of kids going out on lobster boat in AM. Meet @ town docks at 8. In? Y or N? LMK!

It was big of her to reach out (even though she had kind of started our fight today). I wondered if Hayden was going, or Samantha. I wasn't sure that the outing sounded like the most fun thing in the world, but I couldn't go anyway. I was working at the library tomorrow for my first time, and I was looking forward to it, actually.

Can't. Work. Thx.

I replied and pressed Send but it looked a little terse. I guess I could have elaborated to match her friendly effort. I could have been normal and said, "Hey, did you know Hayden Jones can't swim?" or "Hey, maybe Samantha Frankel isn't so bad," or even, "Bud's a pretty nice guy." But none of it seemed right for the moment. As an afterthought, an appeasement, I added:

Seen Indigo Darling yet?

Then I pressed Send again and went to bed.

So it seems like almost everyone in town *has* seen Indigo Darling, up close and personal, except me.

But first, let me back up.

It turns out I am really good at Story Time. Janet told me so, in case I couldn't tell from the little kids' behavior today (though I could). The books Janet had given me to read to them were awesome, which certainly helped. There was *Don't Let the Pigeon Drive the Bus*, and *Blueberries for Sal*, and *What Pet Should I Get?* and *Harry the Dirty Dog*, and I read them all in funny voices and acted them out, and encouraged the kids to participate, and we sang songs and marched around, and I had a blast. And guess what? So did they!

Whenever it started to seem like they might get out of control, I used some of Bud's crowd control tactics, like calling a kid by name, or guessing at what someone might be doing behind my back, and pretty quickly I had them all eating out of the palm of my hand, if I do say so myself! Harry Potter the cat was my co-star, and by the end, he was sitting on my lap while I read one last, peaceful story (*The Little House*) to the kids to settle them down before their parents came for them. I wanted to take a photo of them and post it so people would know about my soft side, and that I had a fun job. But Martin's comments about social media using me still rang in my ears, so I resisted.

It was time for me to go just as the last toddler was being picked up, and Janet gave me a hug.

"Selena, you are a godsend! I am so thrilled by how great you were with those kids today. Thank you!"

I smiled. "It was really fun. It doesn't feel like work to me at all." Unlike Junior Lifeguards, I wanted to add.

"I can't wait for your return on Friday. Thanks so much!"

I gathered my things and pulled out my phone to check in. I had a missed call from Hugo, but I'd see him soon enough so I blew that off. Instead, I checked my notifications, which were rolling in like crazy. I hadn't even made it down the steps of the library before I had to sit down. Instagram, Snap and Facebook were blowing up: the Junior Lifeguard kids had all gone out on that lobster boat this morning with a friend of Bud's, and guess who they'd met on the docks?

Indigo Darling!

The group photos and individual photos of

the Junior Lifeguard kids who'd gone (including Hayden, Samantha, Jenna, and even Ziggy) were splashed across all of my social media, all featuring an adorable Indigo Darling, front and center.

All of my joy and pride at the successful morning I'd just had dissipated, as I stared listlessly at my phone. I'd missed out, and I was the one who probably cared the most about meeting him, too. What a bummer.

I unlocked my bike from the rack and pedaled slowly to the pet store, where I bought a small bag of kibble and two little plastic bowls (one for water, one for food) for Oscar. Then I stopped for a bagel and ate it standing at the counter in the coffee shop. I already had my lifeguard gear, so when I finished eating, I pedaled off to the beach, slowly and sadly, feeling totally left out. It was hot today and the air was still except for the drone of hedge clippers, cicadas, and the occasional prop plane in the sky. I was sweating before I'd even gotten halfway to the beach.

At Lookout, I changed and brought the bowls

(one filled with food) out from the locker room in the pavilion. I was avoiding the other kids until the last possible moment. I couldn't fake being happy for their morning of excitement. But when I reached the deck of the pavilion, what seemed like my entire Junior Lifeguard class was sitting there, eating their lunch together. It turned out they'd gotten a bunch of lobsters from their outing and the Clam Pot had cooked them and made lobster rolls for everyone.

"Leeny!" called Ziggy, waving me over.

I was worried I might cry if I went right over there. I gestured to the cat bowls in my hand. "Hang on," I said. I went inside to get water from Hugo for Oscar.

"Hey! Did you hear . . ." said Hugo with a huge grin, as he came to greet me at the counter.

I rolled my eyes. "Yeah, yeah, all the kids met Indigo Darling on the docks this morning. And I missed out yet again."

Hugo's eyes shone with excitement. "But he was just here, too! Look!" He pulled his phone out of his pocket and showed me a selfie he'd taken at this very spot, of him and a smiling Indigo Darling.

"I called you!" said Hugo. "I wanted you to get down here to try and catch him, but I knew you had your first day of work. I'm sorry."

I felt my eyes well up. This was more than I could take. "Everyone's met him but me! I'm sure I never will, now!"

Hugo came around the counter and put his arm around me. "Hey, sis. Don't cry. You saw him first, before anyone, don't forget. The other day in the parking lot."

I scoffed. "Yeah, but I didn't even know it was him, so it doesn't count. Plus I didn't get a photo, so it's like it never happened."

Hugo took his arm off my shoulder and looked at me with a squint. "Seriously? Just because you don't document it, it isn't real? That's kind of lame, don't you think?"

I sniffed away my tears and tossed my hair. If he wanted to fight, I could fight. "You don't need to judge me, Mr. Self-Righteous. Whether it's right or wrong, it's true. If it's not caught on film, it's *like* it didn't happen. You can't argue with that."

"I do argue with that," he said. He took the bowl and went to fill it in the sink behind the counter and he came back. "And you should be ashamed of yourself for thinking like that. There's so much more to life than showing off to the public. The best things in life aren't documented on Snap or Instagram for all the world to see."

"Oh yeah, Saint Hugo? So then why did *you* get a photo with Indigo Darling?"

With that zinger, I spun on my heel and strode out, right around the corner to find Oscar. Luckily, he was there and he was alone. I put the bowls down and gave a few sniffs to rid myself of the tears I'd almost shed in the Clam Pot just now.

Oscar ate greedily and purred loudly. I dared to reach out and stroke his back and he let me, only stiffening briefly when I first touched him. I looked for any signs of fleas or diseases, thinking cats need checkups just like people do. I wondered if I could catch him and take him to a vet, just to be sure he was healthy, even if he didn't come live with me. I'd have to think up a plan. I sighed and left Oscar to eat in peace.

Outside on the dining deck, the lifeguarding kids were all still wild with their morning of excitement. Hayden was holding court, talking about how he'd spied Indigo under his fishing hat and dared to go over and say hi.

Samantha had apparently been very brazen, too. She'd met Indigo twice before at some star-studded fundraisers back home in London (of course), and had immediately approached him and begun making connections until they were apparently laughing and chatting like long lost friends. That really irritated me.

Even Jenna was thrilled at meeting him, and Ziggy, and they usually dislike rich and successful people on principle, just because of how they live (Ziggy goes crazy at multiple home owners and private jet riders, because of their carbon footprints, and Jenna thinks they are spoiled). Everyone was recounting their stories and showing their pics, and it was just so annoying and unfair! None of them even want to be actors when they grow up.

It was time to head down to the training area. I sighed heavily and indulged in some more self-pity. *I'll never meet Indigo Darling. I'll never become a star,* I thought morosely. *I'll be stuck here on the Cape forever.*

"Hey, Leeny!" It was Piper, coming up behind me. She put her hand on my shoulder as we walked. "Sorry you missed the big star. I know how important that would be to you."

I almost cried. Piper was a true friend. "Thanks, Pipe. It is such a bummer. I just can't shake it. I feel like I missed my big break."

Piper smiled. "I wouldn't go that far. It's not like he's Mr. Famous Movie Director. But it would have been fun to see him. Anyway, who knows? Maybe we still will!"

I shook my head. "I know it sounds awful but it just really bugs me that everyone else got to see him, and that, like, Samantha Frankel is *friends* with him."

Piper nudged me with her elbow. "I know. But come on: you can't compete with her, that's a losing battle. And I'm sure you'll see him. Hey, want to sleep over tonight and we could go to town and look for him? We haven't done anything fun all week and *hello?* It's summer!"

I sighed. "Okay. Thanks, Pipe. I'll check with my mom later."

"Great." Piper smiled and her bright blue eyes twinkled. "Now let's see what fresh torture Bud has lined up for us today."

The fresh torture was this: After all our hideous warm ups, and a boring lesson on how to strap someone to a rescue board, I was assigned to my partner for the day. And it was Samantha Frankel.

7

Buoyed Up

Samantha and I were quiet on the bike ride to Queensbury Beach. Not only had Bud assigned us together, but he'd also given us the most deathly boring of all assignments. We'd have three hours to fill on a beach without waves, that was always devoid of beachgoers, where there was no one else except the senior lifeguard Mr. Talbot, who was a science teacher at the high school during the year and a lifeguard during the summers. He was nice but a full-fledged adult, so not exactly cool to chat with. It felt like a punishment, though I knew Bud well enough by now to know that it was random, just unlucky.

I could not think of anything to talk to Samantha about. I was paralyzed by our awkward conversation from the day before, I didn't want to discuss Oscar because that was a nerve-wracking topic, I was upset about missing out on Indigo Darling, so I didn't want to bring that up. In short, I was tongue-tied and unhappy.

When we reached the empty parking lot at Queensbury, Samantha finally broke the ice, saying, "Holy ghost town, Batman!" They were the first words uttered by either of us on the seven-minute ride.

"Yeah," I agreed. *Brilliant reply, Selena. Just brilliant,* I thought.

We locked up our bikes and walked down on the wooden boardwalk the town laid through the dunes.

"I bet the ice cream truck doesn't even stop here!" said Samantha.

The ice cream truck is a beach tradition on the

Cape. When you hear the jingly tune coming into the parking lot, you automatically turn to your parents and start begging for money, even if you're not hungry. At the more rustic beaches, it was the only place to get a cold drink without leaving to go back to town.

I smiled a little. I wanted to think of a witty reply but I was too nervous.

We trudged across the sand toward the shallow water. The sand was hot underfoot and the heat seemed to radiate up from it. We said hi to Mr. Talbot who was on duty under an umbrella despite his already dark skin, with a big straw hat over his short dreadlocks, reading a thick book called *The Origin of the Species* by Charles Darwin. There was not one single other person on the beach.

"Hi, kids! Put on some sunscreen. The sun is deceptively strong today," he said.

I took a minute to apply some more sunscreen, mostly just to fill the time. Mr. Talbot put his nose back in his book and it was just me and Samantha again.

"Anything you'd like us to do?" asked Samantha helpfully. It was weird for me to see her in the role of underling. Kind of like the old movie *The Prince and the Pauper* where the prince and commoner swap places.

Mr. Talbot tucked his finger in his book to hold his place. "Oh, right. Hmm. There's not really much to do here. Certainly not anyone to watch in the water! The last pair of Juniors cleaned up the trash yesterday . . ." He tapped his book cover with his thumb as he looked around. "Actually . . ." His eyes lighted on Reynolds's Island, across the channel. "You could bring our emergency kayak over to Reynolds's for me and swim back. Just tuck the kayak up in the dunes and leave it there? It's for people whose boats break down or who might swim out there but not have the energy to swim back."

Like me, I thought grimly. *I'm actually the kind of person who would need the emergency kayak.* But I wasn't about to admit it. I couldn't bear to give Samantha another reason to think of me as inferior to her.

"Fun!" said Samantha. "We're on it!"

My stomach clutched and my palms went cold. It wasn't too far but distance swimming isn't really my thing, obviously. But how could I tell Mr. Talbot that? And what would Samantha think? I mean, I know I *look* like a lifeguard in my red suit and I did pass the test, but I'd be mortified to admit my weakness to either of them.

"Let's go!" said Samantha, practically skipping to the dune's edge down by the water where the kayak had been drawn up on shore.

I hesitated but Mr. Talbot had hauled the paddle out from under the lifeguard stand and was handing it to me. "It's a quick ride. I'll think of something more challenging for when you get back," he said apologetically.

"Thanks," I said, and I tucked it under my arm like I'd done this a million times. *More* challenging? I'd never even kayaked before, never mind swimming the channel!

"Hey, life jackets!" Mr. Talbot called after us, holding two orange life vests aloft, one in each hand. I hot-footed it back across the sand to get them, and resumed my march to the kayak. "And stay together," he cautioned.

Over in the dunes, Samantha had grabbed hold of the toggle at the nose of the kayak and was trying to drag the small boat toward the water. I located the toggle on the back end and lifted. We crunched over the piles of dried seaweed and over the rocky fringe of the water, I with the paddle clutched awkwardly under one arm and the two life vests hooked under the other. Samantha wasn't carrying anything.

She steered the boat into the water and pulled the kayak until the water under it was about a foot and a half deep. Then she clambered in, the boat rocking and tipping as she sat down.

"Let's go! Come on. Chop, chop!" she cried. "All aboard!"

The boat was moving away from me so I had to kind of chase it and steady it. It was hard for me to climb in with everything I was holding. I was all wet and didn't want to slosh too much water into the boat, either. I tried one foot and then the other, but I couldn't figure it out.

"Here, give me the paddle. Now, butt first!" ordered Samantha.

I was going to have to ask for help. "Can you take the life jackets too, please?"

"Life jackets! Is he kidding?" Samantha scoffed. Darting a quick glance up at Mr. Talbot, she saw that he was engrossed in his book, so she flung the life jackets back onto the dry sand. "Who needs these things? We're only going a hundred yards!"

My jaw dropped. Not only was she disobeying a lifeguard (who was also a teacher), but I wasn't so sure I could get back without a life jacket.

"Um . . ." I glanced up on the shore at the orange heap.

"Get in!" shouted Samantha, so I did as she said, the kayak tipping precariously as I lowered myself onto the seat. And then I was in, swinging my legs in over the side and into the slot. I tried to ignore the warm, dirty seawater puddling at my feet in the kayak and the sense of dread and vulnerability I felt without the life jacket.

"Woo hoo!" Samantha cheered, and she pumped her fist in the air. "Junior Lifeguards rule!" she looked over her shoulder at me and laughed. I forced a little laugh just to be social. I'd made it onto the kayak. Now I just had to make it to the island and make it back. No problem.

Samantha held the paddle across her lap and began expertly dipping it in the water to push us along, first on one side, then on the other. We began to pick up speed.

"So I guess you've done this before?" I said, breaking the silence.

She turned and looked at me and said wryly, "It's not exactly brain surgery," so I clammed up again.

I dangled my fingers in the water and felt it grow cold as we left the shallows and began crossing the bottomless, navy blue water of the channel. I didn't look down; I was too intimidated by how deep it might go.

The channel had been dug probably over a

hundred years ago for big fishing boats coming to and from the port out to sea, but nowadays it was mostly used by recreational boats: Boston Whalers and the occasional swanky Hinckley that passed through here on their way to island picnics or out for some tubing. But today, because it was a weekday and still early in the season, it was quiet.

"Look at that current!" said Samantha, impressed.

"What?"

She tipped her paddle toward the water. "See how fast it's moving? The tide's going out and the water rushes through the channel."

"Oh. Wow."

"Yeah. That's strong," she said. "Hey, so how's Project Kitty today?"

I guessed we were in chummy mode now, since we were alone out here with no one to see her talking to me.

"Pretty good," I said. "I brought him some food and water in little bowls today and he let me pet him while he ate." I was pleased to report this to her, as if it was something I'd accomplished.

"Aw, he's such a cutie. I wish one of us could keep him."

"Yeah. I just wish I could get him to see a vet to make sure he's healthy."

"I could help with that! We could make my nanny Nigel take us, that self-absorbed pretty boy. Might as well make him work for a living for a change!" she cackled.

I was embarrassed and I didn't know what to say. I wondered if Samantha felt *my* parents worked hard enough. "Okay."

"Sorry, but he is just here for the partying. All he wants to do is head off to P-town to go dancing every night. Then he sleeps all day. I don't even know why my parents have him come here. It's more like *us* looking after *him*."

I wanted to change the subject. "What's your sister doing this summer?"

"Coding. Yuck." Samantha looked back at me and rolled her eyes. "She has a tutor who comes to the house and they just have hack-a-thons all day.

She just adores it. She's going to be the next Edward Snowden."

"Wait, a coding tutor? Does he have blue hair?"

"Yes! How did you know? Did you see him coming up the drive?"

I winced; I thought we were ignoring our co-living arrangements. "Oh, no. Just . . . I've heard of him before." Darn it! Did I have to share everything with the Frankels? My house, my parents, my friends, my summer program, and now my tutor, too? *Ugh!*

"So let's make Nigel help us with Oscar!" cried Samantha.

"Um, okay. Will he?"

"Nigel will do anything I tell him to!" said Samantha.

I winced, wondering if she realized how bad that sounded and wondering if she felt the same way about my parents.

The kayak crunched against the rocks on the shore of Reynolds's Island. Samantha hopped out and I kind of flopped out and lolled in the warm shallow water for a minute. She grabbed the toggle again and began dragging the boat up toward the dunes to stash it. She had actual muscles in her arms that popped as she used them. I wondered if she did a lot of planking and bear-crawling in her free time.

I stood and turned back to look at how far we'd come. I was surprised to see how far away Mr. Talbot looked from here. The island didn't seem like it was that far off the beach but we'd actually come a fair distance; probably about two hundred yards. I couldn't even make out the lumpy orange life vests on shore.

Reality sunk in. I was going to have to free swim that whole way back, with nothing to support me.

Samantha returned from the dune and stood with her hands on her hips to survey the scene. "We'll have to swim at that jetty in order to fight the current and the tide, otherwise it will carry us way left of Queensbury beach," she said, pointing with her hand in a karate chop toward the other side, but on an extreme diagonal.

"Um, what?" I was stalling for time. I did not want Samantha to see what a bad swimmer I was.

"Let's go!" Samantha crashed through the water for about ten yards until the shore dropped off into the deep channel and then she flopped backward with her arms spread wide. I was too paralyzed to move, or to tell her that Mr. Talbot wanted us to stick together. I'd only be holding her back.

"Come on, Selena!" she cried, swimming away without me. Samantha really was a beautiful swimmer. Her strokes were long, strong, and even; nothing like my sloppy strokes. Samantha was getting further away with every second. I was going to have to let her see how bad I was at swimming or she'd be on the other side before I even started.

"Come on, slowpoke!" she cried, then she porpoised under water and disappeared. I stood in place to watch for her to reemerge, and when she did, she was way farther out. "This is awesome!" she called. She began heading toward the jetty way to the right.

Where she was going made the swim look way

longer. There was no way I was going to add all that distance to my swim. It just wasn't practical for a weak swimmer like me. I'd just go straight across. I set my sights on Mr. Talbot as my destination mark, then I told myself firmly: "Okay, Selena. Forget about what Samantha thinks. Just do this. Just sing a song in your head and go!"

I pushed off the sandy island shelf and into the open water, forgetting everything Bud had taught me in my swim lesson last night. I was kicking in a panicky, plunky fashion and breathing shallowly. The water was suddenly so deep and it was very, very cold: like, cold enough to take even more of my breath away.

I began to do the breaststroke, popping my head up and down out of the water, but I wasn't really getting anywhere. The current Samantha had shown me from the kayak was real, as was the wind. And I guess the pull I felt underneath me was the tide going out. Each time I surfaced, I looked for Samantha to mark where she was. She wasn't too much further ahead of me, but she was much further to my right. Mr. Talbot was still ahead of me, but a tiny bit to the right of where he'd been when I started. Oh, why did I have to be such a weakling!

A part of me knew I should swim freestyle; despite my breathing difficulties, it did propel me through the water faster than any other stroke could. I tried to sing in my head but the pacing felt hectic and my breathing was off, even doing the breaststroke.

I decided to flop on my back and backstroke for a while to settle myself down. I bobbed in the water and tried to take powerful strokes as I stared at the calming periwinkle sky. I tried not to think of what kinds of creatures might be sliding beneath me in the depths below, and I pulled with all of my might against the water and the wind. Finally, I felt calmer and more in control, so I flopped over to try a little freestyle. But when I did I could not believe my eyes. Not only was I now *way* to the left of Queensbury beach and not even one foot closer to shore, I was heading out toward the open sound, carried along by the tide and the current. My pathetic attempts to swim against it were only tiring me out.

Samantha had gained distance and was now way to the right of me, not even within shouting distance.

"Hey!" I called weakly. I splashed my hand on the water in frustration. *Don't be passive,* I scolded myself. "Hey!" I called as loudly as I could. Samantha did not look back.

Okay.

I tried waving my arms at Mr. Talbot, but his head was bent down, reading his book. All right. The only thing I could do was keep moving.

I thought again of Bud's advice on strong kicks and breathing. I rebooted the soundtrack in my head, put my face in the water and began to swim hard, for real, doing freestyle. I worked and worked but every time I checked where I was, I was further out to sea and not any closer to the shore. I could see there was a buoy with a light on it coming up, and I realized that I'd seen it from the shore earlier and it had looked so far away. Now I knew all I would have to do was float in the current and I'd be pulled right to it. It was my best bet. I got on my back to float for a bit to save my strength and let the water pull me.

But I guess the current or tide or whatever gained strength as it came through the narrow mouth of the channel, because when I flopped back onto my stomach to see how much further I had to go, I saw that I'd already passed the buoy by ten yards. I tried to swim back toward it but I was swimming in place. Oh, how I longed for even the slight help a life jacket would have afforded me. I was angry at Samantha for throwing them back but even angrier at myself for letting her. I should have started swimming when she started swimming. I was so worried about her seeing my bad skills that I'd waited too long and I'd lost my "buddy." By trying to be cool, I'd endangered myself.

I began to panic. I didn't want to think about sharks or drowning but suddenly they were *all* I could think of. There was another buoy about fifty yards ahead of me, but I'd be almost around the corner by then and I didn't think anyone would ever find me all the way out there. I accidentally gulped some water and began to choke.

"Stop it!" I scolded myself out loud. I began to pray. My only goal was to reach that buoy. Never mind getting to shore at all; the buoy would be my salvation.

I focused on swimming across the current; I needed to harness its direction to pull me where I needed to go. Now I understood what Samantha had meant when she'd pointed way right of the beach with her karate chop. You have to over-compensate for where the current wants to drag you. I focused on this and pretty soon, I found myself within grabbing distance of the buoy.

"Okay, Selena. You can do this!" I told myself out loud. I tried to think of a movie to inspire me but all that Hollywood stuff seemed so stupid right now. This was real life. Maybe even life or death, though I couldn't let myself think like that. I was starting to shiver in the deep cold water. I was coming along, coming along, and then I grabbed the buoy, just in time! I felt the current grab my legs and try to keep pulling me, but I held fast with all of my might.

The buoy was a small, white metal can rising on a pole out the water, and it was painted in a green band on the top. I held on and tried to spin around to see how far I'd come. As I pulled myself around, I almost lost my grip and I panicked and suddenly thought I might faint.

"Okay. You are okay," I told myself.

And suddenly I heard my name. Was I imagining it?

"Selena!" It was a man's voice. It took all my strength to turn to see where the voice was calling from. "Selena!"

It was Mr. Talbot in a kayak. He was zooming toward me on the current. I saw him stash his paddle across his lap and reach out to grab at the buoy but the tide shot him past me!

"Mr. Talbot!" I cried in relief. But as he passed me I burst into tears.

"I'm coming back around!" he called over his shoulder.

I clung to the buoy for dear life, sagging hopelessly as I felt my energy and strength drain from my arms. I closed my eyes and rested my forehead against my arms. I don't know if I started to sleep or what but what felt like seconds later a powerful arm had grabbed me, and Mr. Talbot was hoisting me gracelessly onto the kayak.

"Selena! Are you with me?" he demanded. I could hear the fear in his voice. I struggled to sit upright but kept slumping in exhaustion.

"Selena, it's alright. You can stay like that. Just speak to me so I know you're okay."

"I'm . . . okay," I sighed in relief. "I'm okay. I'm okay." I closed my eyes in gratitude at being saved and fell into a stupor as Mr. Talbot's strong arms blazed us back to shore against the current that had felt so insurmountable.

Before I knew it, we had reached the beach. Strong hands reached out to lift me off the boat. I opened my eyes to thank Samantha for helping me, and found myself staring into the eyes of Indigo Darling.

What else could I do?

I fainted.

Recommitted

I woke up on a towel in the shade under the life-guard stand, with Bud Slater crouching next to me.

"Selena? Selena? Wake up, honey. Wake up."

I fluttered my eyes open and tried to sit up.

Indigo Darling!

"What? What . . . ?"

Bud patted my arm. "You're okay. You just had a nasty experience, but everything's going to be fine. I had to call your dad. He's coming to pick you up." Bud shook his head angrily. "This shouldn't be a swimming beach. I've been telling them for years it only takes one drowning . . ." He was beginning to rant.

What about Indigo Darling?, I wanted to interrupt him and ask. *Had I dreamt that?* I tried to sit up.

"Just stay resting here. No getting up yet. You've had quite a shock. Just let your strength come back."

"Selena?" Samantha rushed to my side. "You scared me to death! I can't believe you survived!"

I was still angry at her about the life jacket, but I was more angry at myself. "I'm an idiot. I should have worn the life jacket and I should have followed you. I didn't know what you meant about the current."

"Oh, bother. I'm so impressed by you, clinging to that buoy before getting washed out to sea! What a spectacle!" Samantha's eyes shone with the drama of it all. Maybe she hadn't even noticed what a bad swimmer I was.

"It wasn't intentional, believe me."

Mr. Talbot hustled over and knelt down next to me. "Oh, Selena, I am so sorry. I just assumed that because you two were lifeguards . . . well . . . I shouldn't have assumed. But why didn't you wear the life jacket I gave you?"

"It wasn't your fault, Mr. Talbot. I should have admitted that my skills are still . . . developing. I'm sorry I didn't wear the life jacket." I wasn't going to rat out Samantha for tossing them, because I was at fault for letting her. "Thank you for saving me," I continued. "That was really scary . . ." I felt my voice begin to wobble and threaten tears, so I swallowed and shut up. But . . . . "Wait, did I imagine it or was . . . ?"

He and Bud laughed.

"Yes, Indigo Darling pulled you from the kayak," said Bud. "He was jogging inland to float back out in the channel but he changed his mind about the swim after he saw what happened to you. Seems the channel has gotten a lot stronger than it was in his day."

"Is he still here?" I asked, half-hopefully, trying to look around beyond the throng of people who surrounded me. I was mortified that a star had seen me in such a state, but I was so desperate to meet him that I didn't even care if I was all bedraggled.

Bud shook his head. "His family was waiting for him at the other end for lunch, so he had to go. He said he looks forward to meeting such a tenacious survivor on a more auspicious occasion." He smiled kindly. I could tell he knew how disappointed I felt.

I closed my eyes and laid back down. Foiled again.

"Okay," I said. "Just taking a little rest now."

I hoped no one could see the tears leaking from my eyes as I turned onto my side on the towel.

My parents were so nice to me for the rest of the day. They both took the afternoon off and after I took a hot shower, I couldn't stop shivering, so they tucked me into their bed in my cozy PJs and under a bunch of quilts and brought me delicious hot things to drink from the kitchen: chicken broth, strong tea with honey, and *horchata*.

"It's the shock, *pobrecita*," said my dad, biting his lip in concern.

"Drink, *mi amor*," said my mom, smoothing my hair back from my forehead in a tender gesture I remembered more from my early childhood than lately. She held a cup of hot *horchata* toward me and I gulped it eagerly.

I saw my parents exchange a glance.

"Selena, about this Junior Lifeguards," my dad began, clearing his throat. "*Tesoro*, perhaps your Mami and I were a little hasty in having this plan for you."

I looked at my mother, who was nodding. "*Si.* Maybe this is not the right thing for you *este verano*. We were thinking . . ."

". . . maybe the acting camp in Michigan," said my dad. "I checked and they could take you for the rest of the session. *Tres semanas más*. Three more weeks left in the session, *querida*."

I closed my eyes and savored the moment of feeling so indulged, so cared for, so understood. I could chuck everything I was currently doing and get exactly what I wanted. No tutor, no lifeguards, so swimming lessons, no job: just a wonderful month of workshops and improv and singing lessons, surrounded by people who shared my passions. It would be so, so amazing.

"Selena?" asked my mom.

But I couldn't stop thinking about my commitment to being with Jenna, Piper and Ziggy all summer on the beach, and Oscar letting me pet him, and how surprisingly nice Bud could be, and my new kind-of friendship with Samantha, and even the stupid bear crawls, and how funny Martin the tutor was yesterday when he was singing about integers to the tune of "Let It Go" from *Frozen*, and how cute the little kids were at the library when I'd read to them.

"Maybe she's gone to sleep," my dad whispered to her in Spanish.

I opened my eyes. "I'm awake. Thank you. That is so nice and so generous. But I don't need to go to camp this summer. I'm staying. And I'm still doing Junior Lifeguards."

Then I closed my eyes definitively before I could see the expressions on their faces.

When I woke up an hour later, Piper was sitting next to me in a chair.

"Hey," she said quietly, and she took my hand.

I smiled. "I'm not dead," I said.

"Thank goodness. I'd kill you if you died!" joked Piper, patting my hand. "How do you feel?"

"Like an idiot," I admitted. I explained to Piper all about the life jacket and Samantha and my being too embarrassed to have Samantha see me swim.

Piper cut to the heart of the matter. "What's it like between you and Samantha?" she asked.

I had to think for a minute. "It's like this: in public, she ignores me. In private, she talks to me, but she's weird and she makes me feel like an idiot a lot of the time."

Piper tipped her head from side to side. "Hmm. So she's hot and cold; sending you mixed signals. Do *you* want to be *her* friend?"

I scoffed. "No, thank you. She's stuck up and spoiled. And she doesn't want to be my friend, either. Trust me."

"I wouldn't be so sure," said Piper. She gestured at a little vase of pink roses that was now on the bedside table.

"Is that from her?" My eyes were wide.

Piper nodded.

"Was she *here?*" I asked. I was suddenly embarrassed. Had she seen me asleep? Had she been in my parents' room?

But Piper was shaking her head. "No. Some guy named Nigel dropped them off."

"Figures. He probably picked them, too." I said. "You can take them away when you go."

Because I couldn't do the sleepover with Piper after all, she and Jenna and Ziggy all stopped by that night and brought me an ice cream sundae from Buffy's. It had all of my favorite things in it: chocolate malt ice cream, bananas, marshmallow and hot fudge, and I devoured the whole thing while we watched two episodes of *Which Way?*, Indigo Darling's old TV series from when he was just getting started in Hollywood.

After, my mother hung out and chatted with us all about how everyone was liking Junior Lifeguards and how the summer was going so far. She can be really fun and relaxed with my friends in a way she isn't when it's just me and her (she's always trying to correct or improve me when it's just the two of us). My friends love hanging with her, especially Piper because she doesn't get to see her own mom as often as she would like.

But this time, my mom ended up really bugging me.

"How is it going for Samantha? Selena tells me she is in your group," asked my mother.

"Mami, please!" I said. "Let's not get into this!"

"Selena, don't be rude. I just want to know." She folded her arms and waited.

My friends looked awkwardly around the

room, I'm sure wishing they were anywhere but in the middle of this conversation.

"Uh, I think she likes it?" said Jenna, finally. "She's a very good athlete."

My mother nodded and sniffed proudly, like Jenna was just confirming something she already knew. "And does she have friends? Are you girls nice to her?"

Again, people looked uncomfortable. "I think so?" said Ziggy.

"Mrs. Diaz, she's not really . . . a natural part of the group, you know?" said Piper.

"She's pretty . . . la-di-da!" said Ziggy in a funny voice. It broke the tension and we all laughed, but not my mother.

"I hope you will include her. She is all alone," chastised my mother.

"Mami, you can't tell my friends what to do!" I wailed.

Jenna cut in before anything had a chance to escalate. "We will, Mrs. Diaz. We're all just getting to know her and to understand our roles and responsibilities at Junior Lifeguards. We will be nice to her, right girls?" said Jenna, looking at each of us sternly, like the team captain she was.

"Right," Piper and Ziggy said, relieved to be off the hook.

"Right, Selena?" said Jenna.

"Right," I sighed.

The next morning at tutor, I asked Martin right off the bat about the Frankels.

"I didn't know you were also tutoring my boss!" I said.

Martin looked at me in confusion. "Your what? I thought you worked here at the library."

"The Frankel girl. Alessandra. Aren't you teaching her to code?"

"Ah, yes. Alessandra. What a bright girl! An excellent student. But why is she your boss?" He was perplexed.

His compliments stung; I was certain he would not call me bright or excellent. "Well, technically she's not. My parents work for her parents. She could be the boss of me if she felt like it, though."

"That sounds silly. I don't think that would happen. She doesn't seem spoiled to me. In fact, quite the opposite. I know she lives in that lovely house, but where are her parents?"

"You can follow them on Instagram and find out! Ha, ha," I said.

"Ha, ha," he replied. "I'm serious."

"Oh, I don't know. They travel all the time for work and whatnot. They live in London mostly."

"That's a shame. That girl is young to be so un-supervised for so long."

I thought of how annoying my mom could be. "Sounds like heaven to me," I shrugged.

"Humph," scoffed Martin. "It's not healthy."

"Well, there is Nigel, the babysitter."

"Hopeless," said Martin. "Useless. But there is that nice Isabel, the housekeeper lady who seems to be in charge when she's there."

"That's my mom!" I cried, my face flaming.

"Lucky," said Martin, unperturbed. "Now that's enough chatting. It's time for math."

When I returned to Junior Lifeguards training, all of the other lifeguarding kids treated me like I was a celebrity myself. Everyone had heard the story of my saving, and I could tell that my friends had really hammed it up. I was surprised there wasn't a pirate with an eye patch or an ancient ghost ship in the story! I corrected them with my very simple version of what had happened, focusing on my own ignorance and my lame swimming skills and not Samantha's tossing the life jackets or swimming on without me.

What I didn't tell anyone was that I was now on fire to become a great swimmer and the best possible lifeguard I could be. I'd seen how easily I might have drifted away to sea and how Mr. Talbot had saved me, and I knew how important lifeguards were in a place surrounded by water. More importantly, I wanted to help myself. Being a strong swimmer was an important life skill and being in great shape was important for anyone, but especially a future star like myself. I had to start treating what was *under* my skin as well as I treated my skin itself, because strength and energy were what would help me in the long run. Acting is very physical and all the perfect skin in the world wouldn't hide a weakness or lack of stamina within.

Before we started training I excused myself to check on Oscar and give him some food. But when I got to the dumpster area, he was nowhere to be found!

"Here, kitty kitty!" I called. "Here, Oscar!" I filled his bowl and rattled the food a bit, and I got water from Hugo inside, but when I came back there was still no sign of him. I left the food and water because it was time for training.

As I walked down the boardwalk to join the crew, I prayed that a coyote hadn't gotten Oscar. I shuddered just thinking about it. But Oscar was crafty—he was a street kitty. He'd gotten himself this far so I was sure he could outwit a coyote. Couldn't he?

Down on the beach, Bud was serious-faced and called us all to order for a long meeting before we trained.

"First," Bud announced "We will have someone from Woods Hole Oceanographic Institute here tomorrow to tell us about currents and tides and other water features and occurrences. Everyone will have things to take home and study and be tested on."

Ugh!

"Now, for today's info session, I'd like to talk about how important it is for us to know our limits, and how important it is to stay with a buddy in the water." Bud chatted for a while and then started on what a necessity it was to leave our reading material and cell phones tucked away when we were on duty, and how important communication and teamwork were when it came to saving lives.

After that, we had to do a half hour of trust work and little drills designed to help us get to know each other's strengths and weaknesses better. I'd been so fired up to work out that by the end of it, I was actually psyched to do some planks and bear-crawls and just not talk anymore. I thought about how the singing had helped me yesterday and during my swim lesson, and I asked Bud if I could bring a speaker to warm-ups from now on.

He agreed to it on a trial basis, noting that there was to be no music ever while we were on duty, and as I turned away from him, Jenna was right behind me.

We'd been getting along better in the past day or two, and she'd been so nice to me last night—just like the usual close friend that I knew and loved.

"What were you just asking him?" she asked curiously.

"If we could have music for warm-ups! Wouldn't it be fun?"

"Yeah. What did he say?"

"He said yes! I couldn't believe it!"

"It's because it was you who did the asking," she said, looking away.

I felt instantly irritated. I couldn't keep boxing

myself in to please Jenna. "I'm sorry, Jenna! I just can't keep holding myself back just so I don't offend you! It's unnatural for me!"

Jenna put her hands up. "Whoa! Calm down! I'm not asking you to hold back. I'm just impressed by how you handle Bud. You're much more relaxed around him and I'm so nervous and I always want to please him and be all perfect, but it's almost like it backfires on me. I get tongue-tied and nerdy. That's all."

I felt a little better, and then bad that I'd over-reacted. "Sorry. I just . . . you know this whole thing's not my skill set. Obviously! If yesterday proved anything . . ."

Jenna rolled her eyes. "It proved that Mr. Talbot is clueless . . ."

I laughed. "It wasn't his fault. I should have spoken up. I knew that swim was way over my head, ha ha. As for Bud, I guess because he saw my weakness from the beginning the bar is really low for me, you know? I'm not trying to impress him. I'm not trying to play the hero role here."

"Like Blake Lively in *The Shallows?*" teased Jenna.

"Exactly!" I laughed at her using my usual technique of referencing a film to explain what I meant.

"And how's it going with Hayden?" she asked lightly, not meeting my eyes.

I looked at her. "How's what going?"

Jenna shrugged. "Just . . . whatever. You know."

"There's nothing between us. No lovey-dovey, no dates, no touching, nothing. In fact, I've kind of been avoiding him." I realized it was true just as I said it. The swim lesson had been intense and embarrassing for us both and now it was like if we didn't acknowledge each other, then it hadn't happened. No matter how cute he was, I think we would have a hard time connecting now that we both felt so vulnerable and exposed.

Jenna's eyes snapped back to me. "Don't you think he's cute?"

"Don't you?" I asked.

She looked away. "Yes. I think he's super-cute. I really like him."

We paused.

"Like, *like him* like him?" I asked.

Jenna nodded.

"So . . . are you like declaring he's yours?" I tried to decipher if what I felt was relief or jealousy.

She sighed in exasperation. "Do you have to make me out to be such a jerk?"

"You're not a jerk. You're just being . . . proactive," I said.

"Are you okay with that?" she asked.

I thought about it. "Well, are you asking me to stay away from him? I can't totally avoid him. I am *friends* with him, and I do think he's cute. And . . . well, let's maybe see who he ends up liking," I added darkly. "It might not be either of us."

As if on cue, down at the shore, Hayden had picked up Samantha, who had suddenly appeared, and he was pretending to throw her into the water. Jenna looked stricken.

"He's a little bit of a player, no?" I said, watching them. "Kind of a bad boy. Like a Christian Bale type."

She nodded and bit her lip. "Yeah. And he's in a bad place in his life right now."

"Really?" I thought of Bud always bossing Hayden around and monitoring his comings and goings. Where were *his* parents? "Family problems?" I asked.

She nodded but didn't say more.

I guess Jenna knew Hayden a little better than I did; maybe she did deserve to be with him. "Hmm. Okay then, I won't do anything to go for him. I promise."

"Thanks," said Jenna, smiling at me in gratitude.

"No touchy feely," I joked.

"Okay. Thanks. And if he ends up liking you, you can have him," she said, but her face was pained as she said it.

"Thanks," I accepted.

Bud assigned us in bigger groups that day, and I was with Ziggy, Piper and Jenna. It was as if he had done it on purpose, to re-bond us four, and we were sent out to Crescent with Jessie, which was the perfect combination of easy and fun, without being boring or hard. We played with little kids in the waves while their moms read on the shore under their umbrellas with their coolers at their sides, and as we chatted, we came up with the idea for an End of Week One Junior Lifeguards party.

9

Oscar Night

My mother was home when I returned from practice today, and I was distraught.

"Mami, the kitten . . . he's gone!" I wailed as I entered our kitchen.

She turned from the stove where she was cooking in her maid's uniform. Sometimes she doesn't take it off at home if she has to go back up to the big house later. I really hate to see her wearing it, but I wouldn't dare say anything. "Oh, *mi amor*. I know how much you cared for him. I'm sorry."

I wrapped my arms around her for a big hug,

and she smoothed my hair and rocked me a tiny bit from side to side. I mumbled into her shoulder, "I just hope he didn't get eaten by a coyote, or trapped somewhere. I hope he isn't suffering . . ."

"Sí, but maybe it is the opposite!" she held me at arm's length and smiled at me. "Maybe he's been rescued by a fisherman who will feed him freshly caught fish every day and give him a little canopy bed to sleep in!"

She made me laugh a little, pronouncing *CAN-opy* as *can-O-py*.

"I hope so," I said, my heart heavy still with worry.

Suddenly there was a knock on the screen door. "Hellooooo!" trilled a female voice.

"Isa?" a man's voice called.

"Hello?" my mom replied, as we both walked to see who it was.

At the door stood Samantha and Nigel, and in Samantha's hand was a pet carrier. My heart dropped. I did not like the sight of Samantha on my doorstep (even though technically it was her doorstep). It was just too embarrassing.

"Good afternoon, Isabel. I am sorry to bother you. I just wanted to see Selena for a moment, please?" said Samantha.

"Hey!" I said, my heart leaping with hope. "Is that Oscar? Is he okay?"

"May we come in?" asked Nigel.

"Of course, of course. Please. Could I get you some *limonata*?" asked my mother, ushering them into the kitchen.

"No, but thanks ever so much. Nigel came to Junior Lifeguards early with me today. We cat-napped Oscar and Nigel took him to the vet. He's just back with the health report. May I?" Samantha gestured at the pet carrier.

My mother nodded and Samantha placed the carrier on the floor. She opened the little door and nothing happened.

"Is he okay?" I suddenly felt frantic to see him. I crouched down and I could see Oscar hiding way back inside. He looked terrified.

"*Hola*, baby!" I whispered. "Come!"

But he was scared and he wouldn't budge.

"Mami, do you have any cheese or something I could use to get him out, please?"

My mom nodded and opened the fridge. She withdrew a little block of cheddar and cut off a tiny slice with a knife. "Like this?" she asked quietly. I nodded and took the cheese from her. Then I crumbled it and laid a little trail from the cage door to the middle of the kitchen floor.

"Oh, Selena. You are smart," said my mother warmly. She crouched beside me and put her hand on my shoulder to wait for Oscar to appear. I could feel Samantha looking at the two of us, but I did not look at her.

At first nothing happened, but then a little nose poked out of the door. Oscar had scented the cheese and began following the trail, delicately nibbling the crumbs as he came.

"Oh! *Qué mona!*" whispered my mom as he exited the carrier. He *did* look cute, and absolutely tiny in our kitchen, even though our kitchen was tiny, too! "He is just a little baby!" she exclaimed.

"The vet said he's about seven weeks old.

Much too young to be separated from his mum," said Samantha. Even though I was grateful she'd taken him, it also bugged me. He wasn't hers to just scoop up (or "catnap"), and it was annoying that she could spend the money on a doctor for a stray cat that wasn't even hers. Or was it? My stomach dropped at the thought of Samantha keeping him.

"What else did the vet say?" I tried to keep my voice level. I wanted to put off the inevitable moment when Samantha told me he was now hers.

"She said he's very healthy—and he is a boy, you were right—and he has no fleas or ticks or mites but she gave him some shots and he needs to go back for more in a month. She said she thinks based on the size of his paws that he's not going to get very big. He'll stay kind of small and slim for good. But she also said people food is fine in a pinch but we've got to be feeding him kitten chow so he gets all the essential vitamins and minerals he needs. Also he needs tick drops on his neck every month."

I nodded. Here it comes.

"So you will take him home with you?" asked my mother.

My heart sank. I looked at Samantha.

Sam and Nigel exchanged a glance. "It's too complicated to bring him overseas. He'd need to be quarantined in the States first for a while and it sounded traumatic. There didn't seem to be a point," said Nigel, raking his fingers through his spiky blond hair.

"So you're just keeping him for the summer?" I said, in agony.

"Actually, we were hoping . . . ." Samantha turned and looked up at my mother hopefully.

My mom looked back at her, "Yes?"

". . . we were hoping you'd keep him," said Nigel definitively.

"Up at the big house?" asked my mother, confused.

Ugh. That would be a total bummer. A tiny cat rattling around in that big house all by himself? I cringed just thinking of how lonely he'd be.

"Actually . . . here?" said Samantha, her voice somewhere between a question and a command.

"Oh!" said my mother, surprised.

I ignored the fact that she was basically bossing my mother to take a pet, and tried to hide my excitement at the idea of the cat coming to live here. Surely my mother couldn't say no to the Frankels!

"But your parents . . . ?" she asked.

"They wouldn't mind. I'm sure. They wouldn't even notice," shrugged Samantha. "And they both had cats growing up. I think. Anyway, he'd be *yours*."

"We don't want to just dump him on you," added Nigel. "I mean, if you don't want him. The vet said he was so cute and healthy, she'd have no trouble placing him with a family."

"*No!*" I cried. "I mean, we want him! Right, Mami?"

My mom's eyebrows were knit together. "He is awfully cute. I'd just need to speak to Ramón about it before I made any decisions."

"The Frankels' credit card would cover all the

medical bills and you could charge the food on the account at Roche Brothers," said Nigel. "And I did buy a litter box for it."

I winced. Talk about awkward. If the Frankels were paying for everything, it would make Oscar their cat.

"Thank you. We would be able to cover any costs," said my mom. "If we kept him, that is."

"Can Oscar stay here tonight at least?" I asked my mom, making my eyes big and innocent like a Japanese Manga character.

She sighed. "*Sí*. I suppose so." She straightened up. "Now, *limonata* and cookies. I insist."

We all had a snack and a drink and watched Oscar explore the downstairs of the house. He was so adorable and curious, it made it less awkward for us all. Hugo came home and he and Samantha created a little obstacle course for Oscar with hidden food and strings to play with, and we all laughed as he figured his way around, eventually learning how to do a short cut and get right to the food.

"He's a smart little guy!" said Hugo, and I felt so proud, like I was Oscar's mom myself.

"He really is cute," said my mom.

I sensed a softening of her resistance. "Want to hold him?" I scooped him up and offered him to her.

"Oh, no. I am not such a cat person. He is fun to look at but I don't need him that close!" she laughed and held her hands out to ward him off. Was she scared of him, I wondered?

"Did you ever have a cat before?" asked Nigel. "Like when you were growing up? We always had one."

"*Sí*, but on the ranch they are working animals. They keep the mice from the crops and the rats from the barn."

"*Eeew!*" I squealed.

"And one time when I was younger than you all, I accidentally got too close to a mommy cat and her kittens and she attacked me. I was so scared and it hurt a lot. I still have a scar," said my mom. She pointed to a very thin white line along her shin that I had never noticed before.

"Goodness! That's fierce!" said Samantha.

"I have not liked the cats so much since then," laughed my mother.

"Well, this is a boy kitty. So no babies to protect," I said. "Maybe you can like him!" We all laughed but I wasn't really kidding.

Though I could laugh, inside I was torn between feelings of extreme happiness that Oscar might come and live with us, and extreme fear that for some reason my father would object and Oscar would be turned over to some other family (or worse, the Frankels). I snuggled him up against my chin and breathed in the warm, wooly scent of his fur. He smelled like a blanket in the sun and the scent made me feel so cozy. Now that he was actually in my house I couldn't imagine giving him up.

Nigel looked at his watch. "We'd best be going now. Thanks so much, Isabel, for the juice and cookies, and for watching Oscar for the night. Just let me know in the morning what you want to do. I can drive him back over to the vet if it doesn't work out." He leaned over to my mom and whispered something in her ear.

She nodded and waved her hand. "No, no," she said gently. "It's okay."

Samantha and I looked at each other and then we stood. Without a word, I handed Oscar to her and she snuggled him close. "I hope you get to stay, you precious little thing." She closed her eyes and stroked his head and he nestled into the crook of her arm and purred.

"He definitely likes you," I said, feeling a spasm of generosity. She nodded and gave him one last cuddle, then she handed him back to me with a heavy sigh. Crossing her fingers she waved them at me, then she turned to leave.

"Hey! By the way, we decided today that we're having a party—like an end of the week celebration for Junior Lifeguards—on Saturday at five thirty. Are you in?"

"In? Are you kidding?" said Samantha over her shoulder. "I'll host it!"

I woke up super early to go see Oscar first thing. My mom had insisted he sleep in his carrier down in the kitchen because she didn't want him roaming all over the house while we slept. I'd had visions of him sleeping on my bed with me, but I didn't want to push my luck by insisting; it was a miracle my mother had let him stay at all. I tried not to be bitter thinking it was because the Frankels had asked.

Unlike my mother, when my father had come in from work, he'd gotten right down on the floor and let Oscar climb all over him. He'd laughed as Oscar sniffed his ear, and he'd grabbed a bit of string and played with the kitten for a good while. My parents wouldn't be rushed—they said they'd discuss it when they went to bed and tell me some-time the next day.

I showered and dressed quickly for the library, then I snuck down the stairs so I wouldn't startle the cat. But someone was already in the kitchen, and as I drew closer I could hear a voice speaking . . . baby talk. It was my mom. I peered around the wall of the kitchen and through the doorway. She was sitting cross-legged on the floor in her running clothes, and she was playing with Oscar!

"Mami?" I asked.

She jumped and put her hand to her heart. "Selena! You startled me!"

I grinned and entered the kitchen, joining her on the floor. Oscar came sniffing over and clambered up onto my lap and nestled in.

"He knows you're his," said my mom with a smile.

"I'm his what?" I asked.

"His mami," she said, reaching over to pat his tiny head.

My heart lurched in hope. "Does this mean we can keep him?" I asked tentatively.

My mom nodded as she continued to pet the cat. "*Sí, mi amor.* Your papi and I agreed. You will need to take care of him and organize the vet and the supplies and everything, but we will keep him. It is okay. *El pequeño milagro.*"

"Mami! Mami! Thank you, thank you!" I flung my arms around her neck and kissed her a million times on her cheek, accidentally dumping Oscar onto the floor in the process. It had to have been the happiest moment of my life, like *ever*! I couldn't wait to post a picture of him on Instagram and on my Snap story and everywhere. I'd do it like a little birth announcement: 'The Diaz Family is happy to announce the arrival of Oscar on June twenty-second! One pound, One ounce. Come by to meet him any time!'

My dad came into the kitchen with a big smile. "You told her?" he asked my mom and she nodded.

I jumped up to give him a hug and a big kiss. "Thank you so much, Papi. This is the best thing ever! Now it feels like we have a real home of our own!" I was so happy and grateful that my parents had given me this little freedom to have a pet even though we lived at someone else's house.

I brought Oscar upstairs and put him on Hugo's

bed to wake him up. Hugo smiled before he even opened his eyes. "Does this mean we're keeping him?" he asked groggily.

"Say *hola* to your new little brother, Hugito!" I said.

"*Hola*, kitty!" said Hugo, opening his eyes and petting Oscar. "Are you psyched?" he asked me.

"Soooo psyched. It's the best thing ever!"

"Are you sure you don't want to change his name to Indigo Darling?" he teased.

"I don't even care about Indigo Darling anymore. I have everything I need."

"Atta girl!" said Hugo. "Now get out so I can get dressed." He kicked at me playfully and I scooped up Oscar to bring him on a tour of my room, his new headquarters.

Oscar hung out while I did my new conditioning routine, involving some mini-planks and attempted pushups, and squats and other strength exercises I'd found online. He'd given me a funny look at a certain point and curled up on my bed for a nap, but I didn't mind. I needed to be strong now for both of us, so I just plowed ahead.

The only thing that was really bothering me was, did I have to be friends with Samantha now so she could come see Oscar?

At work, we only had four kids dropped off because it was a gorgeous beach day: warm and still with just a gentle cool breeze.

"Enjoy these sunny days while they last!" joked Janet to me.

She handed me a stack of books and I read to the kids for a bit, and we did puzzles and some dancing, and then as we began to wind down, some of the moms came back and watched for a little while. I might have hammed it up some with voices in the books, but it was super-fun and the kids got really into it.

At the end, one of the moms came to claim two of the kids and she asked if I ever babysat. I saw

Janet raise her eyebrows and smile at me from her desk, as if to say, "See? I told you!" I answered that I'd love to babysit and she introduced herself and her kids (She was Melinda, and her kids were Tyler and Emma) and booked me for Friday evening, borrowing a post-it note and a pen from Janet to write down her address.

"Shepherd's Path!" I said, reading the address. "Maybe I'll get to see Indigo Darling! That's where he's renting a house, I hear."

She laughed. "Maybe! See you then!"

I worked harder than usual at Lifeguards that day, and I have to attribute it to the music (as well as my newfound mania for safety and fitness). I'd brought my little waterproof speaker and played my "Get Psyched" playlist for warm-ups, and it really motivated me. I don't think I was the only one who felt that way, either. Everyone had a very upbeat tempo that day and as we worked hard, we also had a lot of fun.

"Nice idea, Ms. Diaz," said Bud towards the

end of warm ups, as he circulated to check in on all of the groups.

"Thank you, Mr. Slater, for letting me do it."

"Bud, we're having a Junior Lifeguards party Saturday night," said Jenna, impulsively. "Would you like to come?" She blushed hard as she said it, as if she was surprised at her own boldness.

But Bud was kind. "Why, I'd love to! My wife and I will come. Just tell me where and when."

"Oh! Wow! Okay, great!" Jenna looked at me in surprise as he walked away. "OMG! I can't believe he said yes!" she whispered, watching him join another group of kids and critique their form.

"Why? Lifeguarding is his life, and he likes us!"

"I know, but still!"

"Jen, also, did you notice you're the only one who calls him Bud?"

Her face reddened again. "What? I am? What does everyone else call him?"

"Mr. Slater. But he doesn't seem to mind that you call him Bud. In fact, I think he likes it."

"Really?" Jenna reflected. "Huh." She seemed pleased now. "Well, I *am* the captain," she joked.

"Ay ay!" I joked back, saluting her, and we giggled.

"Now drop and give me twenty," she commanded.

"And me, too!" said Hayden, joining us.

"No, *you* drop and give *me* twenty!" said Jenna to him with a grin.

I hadn't really spoken to Hayden since swim practice the other night. Today he looked better than ever, unfortunately. His tan continued to deepen, which made his eyes look darker and his hair lighter. His clothes were all sort of worn out so you could see his muscle definition through the thin cotton of his tee shirts. I was regretting the promise I'd made to Jenna and had to make my hands into little fists so I didn't reach out and touch him.

He and Jenna started to joke around about who was the boss of who and I wanted to gag, so I left. Samantha was standing by the lifeguard stand, and I went over to join her.

"Hey!" she said. She seemed pleased to see me, acknowledging me in public for basically the first time.

"Thank you so much for everything with Oscar. My parents are letting me keep him."

"You're so lucky!" she cried, and she caught me off guard by grabbing me in a hug. I hugged her back. What else could I do?

"May I come by later and play with him?"

"Uh, sure. *Mi casa es su casa!*" I joked nervously, but then felt like a fool because my house actually *is* her house, of course.

"Thanks," she said. "What do I need to do for the party on Saturday?"

We discussed the menu and who we'd ask to bring what, and we made sure to make a general announcement at the end of the day so that all the kids knew they were invited and where and when to go and what to bring. Jessie offered to be lifeguard on duty at the Frankels' pool, in case kids wanted to swim, and other kids offered to bring hot dogs and buns, chips, brownies, cold drinks, and more. I was in charge of bringing an appetizer and the playlists. Ziggy was bringing hummus and crackers, Jenna would bring some of the famous baked goods from her family's farm stand, and Piper was bringing her grandmother's potato salad.

"So, the Frankel Mansion on Brookfield!" joked Ziggy. "Swanky!"

I didn't say anything. With the recent news of Ziggy's origins, she wasn't really in a place to say anything like that, but of course she had no idea.

"It's gonna be epic," I said. "The Frankels throw good parties. I should know." Because of the Oscar thing, I felt more comfortable about myself and my family's role at the Frankels'. And I guess it was starting to seem like Samantha and I might even become friends.

"Hey, Selena!" called Samantha across the group. "Do you think your mom can help out Saturday night?"

Oh. Maybe not that comfortable. My face flamed. I looked around to see if anyone had heard, and by anyone, I mostly meant Hayden. But he was down at the water chatting with Bud, well out of earshot.

"Um, I'll ask her," I replied.

"Great. Thanks!" said Samantha, turning away.

"Nice," said Ziggy. "Very convenient to have live-in help."

"She didn't mean it that way, I'm sure," said Piper, smoothing things over. "She just meant it like, 'your mom's around, can she help.' I bet she'd ask her mom if she was here, or even my mom."

"Hmm," I said. I couldn't exactly picture Imari Frankel at the grill flipping burgers. The tiny bit of warm fuzzy feelings I had been having for Samantha had just cooled a bit.

On Duty

For my babysitting job Friday night, I dressed for the part of American Teen Babysitter. I had on cute white cut-offs (not too short), a comfy blue gingham button down from Vineyard Vines that I'd gotten for my birthday, my hair up in a bun, and Keds. I'd brought a bag full of coloring paper, markers, three old DVDs from when Hugo and I were little and liked Disney, and a sock puppet I'd made in drama class last year.

I rode my bike to Shepherd's Path and arrived a few minutes early. Piper was going to be babysitting for her regular family and they were also on Shepherd's Path, so we hoped to be allowed to get all the kids together for a little playtime at some point that evening.

The houses were all pretty but they were smallish and close together on this little cul de sac just past the town beach—fun family beach shacks, not the mansions we have over on Brookfield. I glanced at the house numbers as I pulled onto the lane, and saw it would be a few houses up on the left. I scanned the driveways for a big black SUV, trying to determine which house was Indigo Darling's—but he must have been out somewhere. As I pedaled along I heard Piper.

"Leeny! Over here!" Piper was waving me over.

Our houses were right across from each other!

"Hi Pipe! Let me go check in and I'll get in touch with you if we can play!"

"Selena, come!"

"Hang on!" I said. Jeez. Didn't she know I was here to work, not to socialize? Piper, of all people!

She waved her hand at me in disgust, like 'go on

then,' and turned back to her kids who were trying to scale her like she was a tree. Whatever. I'd be there in a minute.

I hopped off my bike and wheeled it over the small bumpy lawn. The grass was dry and the house was a little weather-beaten, but it looked charming and easy and I was actually glad not to be at some snobby rental house where I'd have to be chasing the kids around with wet-wipes all night and keeping them from breaking anything. There was a beach wagon at the front door and a bunch of flip-flops. I rang the doorbell and looked around. Shepherd's Path was actually a cul de sac, with all the houses facing each other around a ring at the end that had small grassy field in the middle of it. It looked like a fun neighborhood. I could hear the kids inside the house and they sounded excited that I was here, which made me pleased. I had debated bringing Oscar but my mother said no way, citing possible allergies and sharp kitten nails and the hassle of looking after him while trying to watch small children. I knew she was right but I also knew the kids would have gone crazy for him. At least I had a bazillion photos on my phone to show them.

The door opened and I turned back with a smile on my face and I nearly fainted. It was Indigo Darling at the door, with the kids at his feet and a big welcoming smile on his face.

"Um . . . oh . . . I think . . . do I have the wrong house?" I stammered.

"Selena!" cried the kids, running out and grabbing my hands.

"Hi Selena, I'm Indigo. Thanks so much for coming." He reached over to shake my hand and I extricated it from one of the children so I could comply.

"I . . ."

His wife bustled into the room, fastening an earring. "Hi Selena! Thanks for coming!" She had a warm, friendly smile, too, that I recognized from the library.

"Hi Mrs. . . . uh . . . Darling. Thanks for having me." I couldn't even look at Indigo. "Hi kids!"

Mrs. Darling gestured at Indigo. "I wanted to

tell you at the library but then . . . I don't know. I guess I didn't want to scare you off!" she laughed.

"Oh, haha. Yeah. Well . . ." I finally dared a peek at Indigo. My knees were shaking and my palms were sweating, but I tried to remain calm on the outside. "You don't look too scary. And anyway, the whole point is you're not even going to be here!" I joked, finding my footing a little.

"Yeah, I try not to bite the babysitters," he said. "It's so hard to find good ones. I don't want to scare them off!"

We all laughed and suddenly I felt more comfortable. "All my friends have seen you all around town and at the lobster boat docks and everything."

"Wait, you're a lifeguard! I know you! You're the one who clung to the buoy the other day! Honey, remember when I got scared off swimming the channel?" He turned to his wife for confirmation.

Now my face was purple, I was so embarrassed. "Yep, that was me. The lifeguard who couldn't save herself!"

Mrs. Darling shook her head. "I can't believe

they even allow swimming at that beach. That current is so dangerous."

"They might close it to swimmers, actually," I said. "I think it'll probably become just a kayak put-in, but they'll leave a guard there to be sure."

"Smart," she said.

"You were very brave. I'm sorry I couldn't stay to say a proper hello that day. We were going to meet my mom for lunch and I was already late." Indigo actually looked apologetic which, of course, was unnecessary.

Mrs. Darling rolled her eyes at him, but she was smiling. "Which we're going to be again if we don't get a move on!" She filled me in on the schedule which she'd also written down, along with their cell numbers, and she gave me permission to take the kids to play with Piper's kids and to get them ice cream if the truck came by.

The kids and I stood at the door and waved goodbye as they climbed into a Ford Escort and drove off. Remembering the other car, I asked the kids what had happened to the fancy SUV.

"Our mom said it was too flashy, so we gave it back to the rental guy and got that one," said Tyler, the older brother, who was around six.

Emma, aged four, nodded, slipping her thumb in to her mouth and looking up at me to see if I'd tell her to take it out. I leaned down and whispered in her ear, "I used to suck my thumb, too." She smiled around her thumb and I knew we were friends for life.

The kids and I had a blast that evening. We ran over to play with the other kids right away and Piper said, "I tried to warn you!"

I shook my head in disbelief and apologized for blowing her off. She said she'd had an inkling that that was who it would be, but she hadn't mentioned it because she didn't want to get my hopes up.

"It's weird because, like, in real life he's just a dad, you know?" I said, mulling it all over. "And his wife is super-mellow and unfancy, and the kids are just . . . kids!"

Piper nodded as we pushed Emma and her little guy on the swings in the backyard.

"Stars. They're just like us," joked Piper, quoting a magazine headline.

"Yeah," I sighed. "But better."

"Did you get a photo?" asked Piper. "You've got to post about it! Or put it on your blog! It will be amazing. Like, up close and personal with Indigo Darling! You can tell all about what his kids are like, and post a pic of what he has in his fridge!"

I was shocked. I turned quickly. "I'd never do that!" I said, but then I saw Piper's eyes twinkling.

"I would hope not!" she said, and I play-socked her.

"Do you know what was the coolest part?" I whispered.

"What?"

"He knew who *I* was. Like, he recognized me, from the drowning incident the other day."

"Seriously?" Piper's eyes were wide.

I nodded. "Indigo Darling knew who I was. Little old me." I couldn't get over it.

"That *is* really cool," said Piper solemnly. "And you only had to almost die for him to know you. Tough to Instagram that kind of moment, unfortunately."

"Shush!"

The evening went by quickly and the kids were still awake when the Darlings came home. Luckily Emma and Tyler were in their beds, but I was singing to them (taking requests) so I didn't hear the car come in the driveway or the front door open. I turned as the Darlings came to the bedroom doorway, and I stopped singing, embarrassed.

"No! Keep going!" said Mrs. Darling. "You're good!"

"Sing 'Love is an Open Door' again, from *Frozen*!" commanded Emma.

I laughed and tickled her. "Haven't you had enough for one night?"

"Sing!" she said, pointing at me.

"Okay, boss." Embarrassingly she reminded me of Samantha just then, but I did as she said. And as I sang, suddenly Indigo chimed in for the harmony, and we sang the rest of the song as a duet for them. It was totally cool and surreal and fun. He was a terrific singer, but I already knew that from seeing him sing on the Academy Awards show one year.

At the end, everyone clapped, including me, and I stood up and high-fived the kids goodbye.

"Selena, when can you come back?" asked Tyler.

"Anytime, buddy. I loved babysitting for you guys."

Emma hugged me and I left to go downstairs with Mrs. Darling while Indigo tucked them in.

"You have a wonderful voice, Selena," said Mrs. Darling, grabbing her purse.

"Oh, thanks. It's just one of those things," I said. I didn't want to get into the whole acting thing because it would have felt like I was shaking them down or something.

"Do you act, too?" she asked, searching for her wallet.

"Well . . . yes. I do." I didn't elaborate.

"Hmmm," she said digging through her purse.

"Oh, if you don't have change, honestly, you can pay me another time. Or, actually it was so fun, you don't even need to pay me. Really," I said, meaning it.

"You are too sweet. No, I have the money right here. I was just looking for one of these!" She pulled a card from her bag and held it triumphantly aloft, and then handed it to me.

"Thanks," I said, glancing at it.

Melinda Bates Darling

Talent Scout

The Walt Disney Company

"Oh!" I said, shocked momentarily. I looked up at her. She was smiling at me.

"We leave this weekend, but stay in touch. You have such charisma and kids obviously love you, plus you've got that great voice. You should be in showbiz, kid!" she joked.

Indigo came plodding barefoot into the kitchen and saw the card in my hand.

"Oh no! She's trapped you, too! Run, run while you still can!" he joked.

I smiled, and Mrs. Darling said fake-huffy, "Selena is a career-minded gal with a lot of talent. She might like to work in film one day."

Indigo grabbed a bottle of water from the fridge and cracked it open. "Honey, according to her friends Selena lives over on Brookfield Lane. She might not need a job at all!" he teased.

I blushed. "Oh. No. Actually, I mean. That's not my house. It's . . ." I gulped. I was so embarrassed but I felt I had to clear up the misunderstanding or Mrs. Darling might never hire me! "Uh, my parents work there. They're the housekeeper and property manager there. It's just . . . we live in the caretaker's house."

"Everyone needs a job, honey, no matter what lane they live on," said Mrs. Darling to Indigo.

Indigo was smiling. "My mom was a motel maid when we lived here. It's honest work. I used to be so embarrassed, though, when she would pick me up on her uniform!" He rubbed his face and shook his head at the memory. "I was such a jerk and she was killing herself to support us."

"Yeah, I know what you mean," I said, shocked that we shared such similar backgrounds. "My mother always says, *No one can make you feel inferior . . .*"

"*Without your consent!*" finished Indigo triumphantly. "My mom used to say the same thing!"

"Eleanor Roosevelt," said Mrs, Darling admiringly.

They walked me to the door and out to my bike, and stood there as I hopped on and got ready to pedal off.

"Are you okay riding home?" asked Mrs. Darling.

"Just fine," I said. "It's not even totally dark out yet. Thanks so much for having me to babysit."

"Thank *you* so much for coming and taking care of our little tyrants," joked Indigo.

"They're adorable. See you soon!"

"Good luck, kiddo," he called, and waved as I pedaled away.

Riding home, I couldn't believe the evening I'd just had. Like I actually could not believe it had happened. I'd met a major celebrity, made money, hung out with my friend, and gained an amazing Hollywood contact—all in one night! Plus I learned that Indigo Darling's beginnings were just like mine. Parts of the night seemed like I dreamed them (singing in the kids' room with Indigo Darling? Seriously?) and parts seemed so normal and familiar (getting paid, saying goodnight at the door). My head was spinning faster than the spokes on my bike and all I wanted to do was curl up with Oscar and tell him everything. The weird part was, I'd just had probably the most exciting and important night of my life tonight and met the most exciting person ever, and there was still no way for me to post about it to prove it.

Would it be enough that just my friends and family and I would know about it? I guessed I didn't have a choice.

Let It Go

It was really fun to have Saturday off after the busy week I'd just had. I couldn't sleep late because I had to get up and feed Oscar and play with him, but I didn't mind. I had my at-home morning, with all my skincare and career maintenance, plus my new fitness regimen. I pinned Mrs. Darling's card on my bulletin board and kept looking at it. Would I actually ever use it?

I spent some time researching the Darlings online. Her job was pretty big—she'd actually discovered a few notable TV stars and she had a lot of mentions on film industry websites. Indigo was super-cute in movies and photos but in real life he was just a dad and a husband—not really crushable. It was weird to think of him as almost two people—the public one and the private one. I think if I saw him on the street as a stranger it almost would be more thrilling than babysitting for him in his house, in a weird way. He'd be just a big star to me, rather than human.

"Selena! Samantha's here!" my mom called up the stairs.

Oh no. I guess she took the *"mi casa"* thing to heart.

"Coming!" I called nervously.

I took a quick look in the mirror and headed downstairs.

"Hey!" I said, not too enthusiastic but friendly enough. I was still smarting a bit from the comment about my mom helping at the party.

Samantha was on the floor with Oscar in her lap. "Hi." She seemed kind of down.

"What's up?" I asked, joining her.

"Oh, I just needed a cuddle."

"Is everything okay?" I asked, having a hard time feeling sorry for her.

"Yeah." She didn't say more for a moment, but I sensed she wanted to. We both patted Oscar for a minute and my mom came in.

"Would you girls like a snack? I have some donuts from town?"

Samantha shook her head, "No thanks, Isabel."

I declined as well and my mom went back to whatever she was doing in the other room.

Samantha sighed. "You're so lucky to have your mom as a mom," she said finally.

"What? Oh. Yeah. I guess?"

Samantha looked at me. "She's always here, right?"

"Well, she goes to town for errands and church, and down the Cape sometimes with her friends for dinner. She's not a *total* homebody, but . . ."

"But she never ditches you or dumps you on anyone else for weeks or even months at a time. She doesn't pay people to be your friend and then never follow up to see if those so-called friends even come home at night from their discos. She doesn't promise you she's coming to visit and then cancel at the last minute, does she?"

I was shocked. "No, she doesn't," I admitted quietly.

"Hmm. Thought so," said Samantha.

"Is everything okay?" I asked.

Samantha sighed. "My parents were supposed to be coming over for a few days. Then my dad had to cancel but my mum was coming 'for sure, for sure to see my little angels'," Samantha mimicked bitterly. "But then some war called or a princess fell off her horse or some flower bloomed in the shape of Santa's head and she had to go on location for the news and she's not coming."

"I'm sorry," I said.

She shrugged. "Whatever. I'm used to it. It's upsetting but what's really upsetting is that I fall for it every time! I should know better! She's not coming! Why do I even ever think she is? I'm such an idiot." She shook her head ruefully.

"No, you're not an idiot at all. You just . . ." I was kind of out of my element here so I searched my mental database of films to pull out some sort of analogy. "You're like Ponyboy in *The Outsiders*. We read it in school and then saw the movie. You're hopeful and loyal and unruined. You can't let her get you down. You've got to stay gold, like they say in the movie. *Stay gold, Ponyboy*. It's not your problem, it's hers."

Samantha looked at me then quickly looked away. "I'm sorry I yelled out the thing about your mom helping at the party when we were at the beach."

I blushed but I tried to stay casual. "Oh, well . . ."

"It was rude of me. I know we don't really acknowledge all this . . ." Samantha made a gesture to encompass us, the room, the property.

"Yeah," I said.

She looked at me again. "I don't think of your mom as like, our maid or whatever," she whispered.

"Well, she kind of is . . ." I said.

"Technically. But it's more like *she's* the boss of *me*, you know?"

"Why yes, I *do* know how that feels!" I laughed and it broke the awkwardness a little.

"I just meant could she help us as a mom, you know? 'Cause I don't really have anyone else here. I just didn't want you to take it the wrong way."

"Thanks." What else could I say? I had taken it the wrong way, but I guess that had kind of been my choice. I could have read the question either way, but I had chosen to feel inferior.

I couldn't believe I was speaking so intimately with Samantha Frankel. This summer was just full of surprises, and it was still only June.

"I'm sorry I kind of intruded on your summer plan. Your mom really thought Junior Lifeguards would be fun for me, too, but I can tell I'm cramping your style." Samantha looked glum.

"What?" I was horrified. Had it been that obvious? "No. Don't worry."

Samantha shrugged. "I just don't have anything else to do if I don't do Junior Lifeguards. My parents didn't set anything up for us and Nigel is hopeless, as you know."

"It's okay. Really. There's room enough for both of us."

"Thanks," she said quietly.

Oscar nestled deeply into Samantha's lap, curled up in a tiny ball and went soundly to sleep. She looked down at him and gave a small smile. "I'm getting a kitten when I get home. And I'm going to take it with me wherever I go. So there!"

My smile matched hers. "You go, girlfriend!"

At four o'clock I went up to Samantha's to help set up. Samantha was pretty organized; she obviously had a lot of experience in party-throwing. She and Nigel and Alessandra had set up the table for the food, put out a ton of candles in big votive jars, and laid out paper plates, napkins and plastic utensils, along with what she kept calling "the bar," though there'd be no alcohol served. They had a tub of ice and a big garbage can for trash.

My mom arrived with the layer dips and chips she'd made as an appetizer, and she bustled around neatening up the pool area: fluffing pillows, deadheading flowers, sweeping dead leaves away, and more. She wasn't wearing her uniform but I wasn't sure if that was her choice or if Samantha had sent word for her to wear normal clothes. Either way, I had to admit it, I was glad. Plus after my chat with Sam, I knew deep in my heart that I could always count on my mom, and not everyone could say the same. I was so glad she was mine, no matter what she wore or where she worked. I was just glad that tonight it was capris and a sleeveless blouse and not a black dress with a white pinafore apron over it.

The guests began to arrive at five thirty and the party was an immediate hit. Bud and his wife came on the early side, and Jessie was there to lifeguard as promised. Hayden had gotten his hair cut and had on a new polo shirt and swimsuit, and he looked sharp but not as attractive to me as before when his hair was shaggy and his clothes close-fitting. Jenna seemed to feel the opposite because she was all over him when they went in the pool. I watched the two of them and felt my stomach begin to clutch in fear as they drifted toward the deep end. But Jessie must've known about Hayden because she blew her whistle and waved them back to the shallow end immediately.

We had so much food! I found myself with a heaping plate and was just tucking into it all when Mr. Talbot appeared. "Selena, I just wanted to say again how relieved I am that everything turned out alright the other day."

"It's okay, Mr. Talbot," I said, patting him on the shoulder. "It was my fault for not speaking up. I was too embarrassed."

He shook his head. "Yes. Well, in a perfect world, none of us would ever feel shame. You can read all about that in the bible! Speaking of which, I won't be reading on the beach anytime soon, that's for sure."

"Good. Live and learn, right?"

"I'm just glad you lived, never mind the learning," he said. "Phew. How's the food?"

"Awesome. I just need to do something about

the music," I said, realizing the playlist was repeating for the second time.

But suddenly Samantha was standing on a lounge chair, tapping a fork against a Snapple bottle to get everyone's attention. I snapped the music off just in time.

"Yoo hoo! Everyone! Hello! Could I just have a moment, please?"

Everyone was quiet and she laughed. "I feel like Mr. Slater up here, commanding the crowd."

Everyone cheered and clapped, with some of the boys yelling "Yeah, Slater!"

"I just wanted to say thank you to Mr. Slater for putting together such a fun group of kids. This is my best summer ever so far, even though we're only one week in. Thanks also to all my new friends . . ." she smiled at me and raised her Snapple bottle in a toast. I raised my plastic cup back at her. "And thanks to Nigel and Isabel, my surrogate parents, for letting us have this party and helping us do it. Thank you all for bringing everything."

I looked at my mom's smile and I felt good for her. She is a kind and generous person and she does her job very well. After my chat with Samantha yesterday, I could see why my mother worried over her and Alessandra, too. There was applause and hooting again and then Samantha quieted us all down. "Now I want to introduce another friend of mine from another part of my life. Some of you have met him already, most of you know who he is. He has agreed to treat us to a song tonight from his new film, so without further ado, I now present to you, Indigo Darling!"

Indigo Darling came out the back door of the kitchen looking handsome in khaki shorts, flip flops and a lightweight plaid button-down shirt, and the place went wild! People were diving for their phones to flip on their video cameras, shrieking and cheering and pushing in closer to see him. He waved and laughed and brandished a ukulele he had with him, as people shushed the crowd to let him sing.

"Ms. Frankel, than you for the invitation tonight. It's great to see so many familiar faces in one of the many places I call home. I love being back on the Cape and reliving the best part of my childhood, and I only wish they'd had a Junior Lifeguards program back when I was your age. Samantha asked me to sing a song for you so I've got one I've been working on for my new movie. It's not quite perfect yet but it's fun. It's called *Heroics*. Here goes!"

Indigo sang so well that I had to take back my non-crushing declaration. At this moment he wasn't a dad or a babysitting client—he was a star, and a gorgeous, talented one at that. I really nearly swooned. By the end of the song, the crowd had picked up the chorus and everyone sang it with him. When he finished with a bow and a flourish, people screamed for an encore and he laughed. Then he quieted everyone down and said, "I'll do an encore but I'm not doing it alone. I have a co-star in the crowd here and she and I have been practicing a song in our down time. Selena, will you come up here and sing with me please?"

I do not remember even walking through the crowd; I must have floated. But suddenly I was standing next to Indigo Darling and his ukulele and smiling, beaming at the crowd. "Sorry to put you on the spot. I just couldn't do it alone!" he whispered. "Ready?"

I nodded and took a deep breath, and we began to sing "Love is an Open Door" in full harmony, laughing as we went along. At the end, we held the final note and Indigo grabbed my hand and thrust it into the air.

"Ladies and gentlemen! Selena Diaz! Look for her in major motion pictures in the near future!" We laughed again as everyone clapped and we high fived.

"Thanks," he said. "You were great!"

"Well, I've had years of practice in the shower," I joked.

Piper came up and said, "Say cheese!" and snapped a picture of us, just as Samantha came running up.

"You two were marvelous! Selena, I had no idea you could sing like that! Indigo, how ever did you know, you clever man!"

We explained the babysitting and the bedtime

singing, and soon lots of people were chatting with us and then because everyone wanted a photo with Indigo, I found myself rotated out of his orbit and back to my dinner plate. My hot dog was cold, but it didn't matter. Piper, Ziggy and Jenna were clustered around me and I was literally walking on air, I was so happy.

My mother came over and swept me off my feet in a hug. "Oh, *mi amor*, you were . . . just magnificent! I am so proud of you, Selena!"

As she put me down I saw Samantha standing just behind her, taking it all in. I reached for Samantha and grabbed her into a three-way hug with my mom. "Thanks for everything, Sam," I said, giving her an extra-tight squeeze. "That was an incredible night."

"Thank *you,*" she whispered into my hair. "Both of you."

That night, I had Jenna, Piper, and Ziggy sleep over. We were all crammed into my room and Oscar, too, though my mom was still making me put him in his crate before I went to sleep each night. It was the one concession I had to make, but it was a pretty small one in the whole scheme of things.

We spent most of the night discussing the fact that Samantha and Hayden had wandered off on a beach walk at the end of the night, and Jenna was alternately furious and despondent.

"I mean, what is *wrong* with him? We were having such a great time and then he does this! It's so weird!"

I sighed and for the tenth time that night said, "He's a troubled kid, Jenna. You can't really go for him."

"I can't help it! I really like him! And I don't like Samantha Frankel. I don't care what you say about her suddenly being nice to you, Selena. She's an egomaniac and she thinks the world revolves around her and her celebrity lifestyle!"

I felt bad not defending Samantha but I didn't pile on the way Jenna did, either. I noticed Piper was quiet, too.

"Did you see what she posted on Insta and Snap?" Piper asked, after being quiet a while.

We all whipped out our phones and there was a second of silence as we located her posts.

My summer best friend sings like a bird with this guy.

#Selena #risingstar #Indigo #notyoureveryday-beachpicnic

"Wow," said Jenna. "It's the video of you two singing."

"You look really good," said Ziggy, peering over Jenna's shoulder since she doesn't have a phone of her own.

Piper pushed play on the audio and our voices filled the room. "You sound awesome, too."

"Two thousand likes!" cried Ziggy. "In an *hour?* How many followers does this girl *have?*"

I took a deep breath. "Look, I'm not gonna lie. That is super-cool and thank goodness I finally got proof that I met Indigo Darling! I admit it's nice to be noticed and it's cool having new 'friends,' but I'd actually rather talk about something else for a while. Let's talk about lifeguarding or cats or something! Just no more celebrities or boy drama, okay?"

"But Selena, you of all people!"

"Sometimes you just need to . . . *Let it Go!*" I yelled, and they all pummeled me with their pillows.

Piper was holding my arm back when suddenly she cried, "Selena! Are you getting muscles?"

I pulled away, breathless from the fight, and flexed my bicep.

"Wow! I think I can see a little tiny bit of definition!" teased Jenna, giving it a squeeze.

"Well, I am a mighty, mighty lifeguard you know!" I crowed.

"Hashtag brave! Hashtag strong!" added Piper.

"Hashtag we will save you!" added Ziggy.

"Not tonight!" I cried, and I went back in with my pillow swinging, careful not to whack Oscar in the process.

THE END

ABOUT THE AUTHOR

Elizabeth Doyle Carey is a frequent visitor to the town of Cotuit on Cape Cod, where she roots for the Kettleers baseball team. Though not a lifeguard herself, she loves swimming at Dowses Beach in Osterville and stopping at Four Seas Ice Cream in Centerville for peppermint stick on a sugar cone.

Please visit

WWW.ELIZABETHDOYLECAREY.COM

to learn about other books Liz has written.

Please visit

WWW.DUNEMEREBOOKS.COM

to order your next great book or to read more about fun stuff to do in Cape Cod and other cool places.

CHECK OUT THESE OTHER JUNIOR LIFEGUARDS BOOKS:

#1

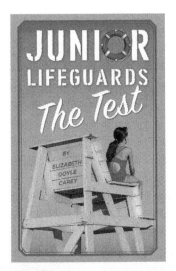

#3

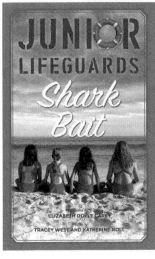

#4

DUNEMERE
Books

WWW.DUNEMEREBOOKS.COM